JENNIE ADAMS

Promoted: Secretary to Bride!

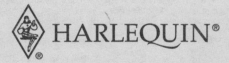

HARLEQUIN®

TORONTO • NEW YORK • LONDON
AMSTERDAM • PARIS • SYDNEY • HAMBURG
STOCKHOLM • ATHENS • TOKYO • MILAN • MADRID
PRAGUE • WARSAW • BUDAPEST • AUCKLAND

Recycling programs
for this product may
not exist in your area.

ISBN-13: 978-0-373-17563-5
ISBN-10:   0-373-17563-9

PROMOTED: SECRETARY TO BRIDE!

First North American Publication 2009.

www.eHarlequin.com

Printed in U.S.A.

Jarrod's gaze dipped, trailed over her shoulders and lower, and came back to her face. "You looked stunning."

Molly should remind him that she didn't fit in, or play down his praise, but instead, she couldn't concentrate on anything but his nearness, and how much she wanted his kiss as his hazel eyes darkened and intent came into his features. Instead she said, "I'm…glad you liked the dress."

"I liked it a lot." His fingers crushed the soft fabric against her skin as he cupped her shoulders. His knee touched hers as he turned more fully toward her. And then his hands were on skin alone— shoulders, back—in the lightest touch that still managed to hold her.

"Why did I never see you?" He whispered the words, as though if he spoke them aloud the spell would be broken. "Why can't I stop seeing you now?"

Molly wanted to be seen. Oh, she did. And she wanted his kiss. And at last his lips came down to cover hers.

Dear Reader,

Sometimes it takes a transformation for us to see what's been in front of us right from the start. That's how it is for Jarrod Banning when he draws Molly Taylor deep into his world to help him sort out a problem—and ends up creating some problems of a whole other kind for himself.

Molly is a special woman, with a unique kind of family. They're all about fairy-tale dreams as a harmless means of escaping from their very ordinary lives. Molly wants only to keep her feet on the ground for everyone, and she's done a good job—despite working for a 'dream boss' for the past three years. She's rather concerned when the rules suddenly change!

I hope you enjoy visiting sunny Queensland with me—the real bits and the fictitious bits—as Molly and Jarrod's story unfolds.

Love and hugs from Australia,

Jennie
www.jennieadams.net

From city girl—to corporate wife!

They're working side by side, nine to five...
but no matter how hard these couples
try to keep their relationships strictly professional,
romance is undeniably on the agenda!

But will a date in the office diary
lead to an appointment at the altar?

Find out in this exciting miniseries.

Memo
To: *Reader*
From: *Harlequin Romance*®
Subject:

Don't miss Jennie Adams's next book,
Nine-to-Five Bride
In April
which kicks off our exciting new trilogy,
www.blinddatebrides.com

And don't forget to make a blind date with

Fiona Harper
Blind-Date Baby
In May

Melissa McClone
Dream Date with the Millionaire
In June!

Visit www.blinddatebrides.com to find out more....

For Laura Hamby,
with thanks for the sanity-saving IM chats,
the daily doses of 'And Today's Whinge Is,' the
title-brainstorming, Cupid, the e-card, the
secret spook and the many M&M's—especially the
peanut butter ones. Consider yourself publicly outed
for niceness above and beyond the call of duty!

CHAPTER ONE

'THAT'S a very generous invitation, Mr Allonby.' An invitation that took geek-girl Molly Taylor completely by surprise. She wanted to assure the man there was nothing wrong with her boss's business whatsoever. There couldn't be! And yet the man sounded so sure.

Molly's gaze moved past him, to the view outside the four-teenth-floor windows of the Brisbane office that housed Banning Financial Services. The Australian sky was as bright a blue as ever, the buildings in the cityscape as tall, the river area below as wide and calm.

Yet a few words from this stranger and Molly's cheerful, all-but-perfect world—if you ignored the few niggling things that weren't so perfect about it—didn't feel quite so bright and secure after all.

What if Allonby was correct, and Jarrod's business was in deep trouble? Allonby was offering her a job, but nothing could compensate for having to walk away from her boss.

'You've taken me by surprise.' She turned back to face the man, smoothed a few strands of dark-brown hair back into the ponytail that had a tendency to slip its moorings when she least expected it. One long, slim finger pushed her funky black-framed glasses farther up her nose as she stared at the middle-aged man.

'I'm sure what you've heard must be some sort of mistake.' It had to be. Molly's boss loved the challenge of investing enormous amounts of money in complicated portfolios for a diversity of wealthy clients, and he was really, really good at it.

'I can only assure you what I've been told came from reliable sources.' Though they were alone in the middle of what was both Molly's office and the reception area for the business, her boss was only a closed door away from them.

A fact Peter Allonby must have considered, because he leaned forward and lowered his voice. 'Even billionaires can get into difficulty. They simply have more at stake if that happens.'

'Ah, well, I'd guessed millions, actually.' And this was *not* a topic for open discussion either way. 'I'm afraid I know very little about my boss's finances,' Molly said primly.

Oh, she knew of the Banning family wealth. Everyone had heard of the long-established Road Ten furnishings. And Molly knew her boss had worked in the family business for some time before striking out on his own. He had told her that much of his history when he'd employed her, but as for his own business situation now—could he be in difficulty? It seemed absurd, but, if he was, how and why?

Molly met Allonby's gaze. 'Could you tell me who gave you this information?'

The man cleared his throat. 'I learned of it from several different people among my society associates and colleagues.'

Not an original source, by the sound of it, nor one he would divulge, but of concern anyway.

Allonby dipped his head. 'My interest right now is in securing your services if the opportunity arises to do so.'

'That's very flattering, though I'm not sure why you would want me "sight unseen", so to speak.' A few short steps took her to her desk. She plopped into the seat and laid her hands on the familiar wood surface.

'I like to keep my eyes and ears open. I've heard Banning mention his satisfaction with your skills.' The man murmured it as though in enticement.

All Molly heard was that her boss had praised her. Her heart suddenly churned with all sorts of silly feelings, the greatest of which was a completely out-of-proportion pleasure that Jarrod had mentioned her at all.

Settle down! So what if Jarrod talked you up at some point? Maybe you'd done a good job of picking up his dry cleaning for him that day!

A light disappeared on the new interoffice phone-system, indicating her boss had ended a call. Another light came on.

Molly didn't recognise this light. She and Jarrod had installed the phone system less than an hour ago. It still needed to be properly coded and labelled, but nothing was ringing…

Allonby came forward. He drew a business card from his pocket and dropped it onto her desk. 'I know Banning would demand a lot of you in this working environment, and I feel you'd be an asset to my company. Consider my offer.'

Molly lifted her gaze from the business card. 'I'll consider what you've said.' Right after she got rid of him and asked Jarrod what the heck was going on.

Allonby smiled politely and left the office a moment later. Molly slumped in front of her computer. Yes. Brave thoughts. Just march up to her boss and start hammering out questions about his finances.

She wanted to contact her mum, or Aunt Izzy or Faye. They worried her sometimes. In fact, they all but drove her demented with their disregard for the future, but they were also her nearest and dearest.

Well, Molly couldn't ring or text any of them. Not now. Not about this. She should stop relying on them so much anyway.

Jarrod's office door opened, and he strode out and caught her eyes with a blazing gaze of grey and green and yellow. His face was tight, his dark hair ruffled as though he'd run his hand through it. A muscle twitched at the base of his jaw.

'Get your bag.' His brows drew down as he waved his hand towards her desk drawer. 'We're going to lunch early. We need to talk.'

'All right. I guess there's nothing here that can't wait.' It was a little early, but her boss was rather irritable, and Molly didn't want to think his need to 'talk' might have something to do with business troubles. Even so, she asked, 'Was—was your phone call with Mr Daniels problematic?'

Molly grabbed her purse, and almost had to trot to keep up with him as he locked them out of the office and strode towards the building's lift.

'Did Daniels's call trouble me?' He gave a bark of unamused laughter as he jabbed the lift's button for ground level. 'You could say that, among other things.'

They had the lift to themselves. Molly watched him from the corner of her eye.

A powerful businessman, in tailored beige trousers and a white shirt with the sleeves rolled halfway up his forearms. His mind for figures and investment strategy amazed her. He was aggressive sometimes, that was true, but when he gave himself to something that mattered to him he did it utterly, and Molly...

Well, it didn't matter how that made her feel, did it? But it made it hard to believe he could get his finances into horrible trouble. She fiddled with the catch of her purse until they disembarked and hit the busy central business district street.

'I heard your discussion with Allonby through the intercom on the new phone-system. His offer of a job.' Her boss bit out this announcement as they made their way through the crowd.

'You did?' She squeaked the words and had to clear her throat. 'I guess I know what that particular red light means on the phone now.'

'Quite.' Jarrod took her elbow to guide her to the entrance of a waterside café. 'Did you—?'

'No.' *No*. She would never simply agree to leave him. 'I wanted him to go so I could ask you what's going on, but I wasn't sure how to tackle it. "I've been offered a job out of the blue" somehow didn't seem the right opening line.'

Nor did blabbing out her internal monologue on the topic, but it was too late for that now, wasn't it?

His fingers squeezed her elbow, and a reluctant huff of grim laughter passed through his lips. 'Perhaps not.'

The squeeze of his fingers was merely an impersonal touch. He wasn't even in a good mood, so there was no need for her to feel all tingly and warm. She should be feeling chilled to the bone and worried.

Actually, she was those things, too. 'Sorry. I babble when I'm uneasy. Mostly I don't, because usually I have good control over the things that impact on me, though I do it sometimes because of Mum, Izzy and Faye. If they're causing me more hassle than usual. But you don't need to hear about that. It's boring family stuff.'

'Your job is safe, and I don't want you leaving the company.' He spoke as she finally wound down. 'How about we start there and work our way through the rest?'

Good idea. 'Thank you. I was worried about that a little, though not hugely, because I couldn't see how you could be in trouble, but I'm relieved.' She was babbling. Again. 'Anyway, I didn't accept Allonby's offer.'

'You won't need to.' Jarrod gave his order. Molly quickly added hers, and her boss paid for the food with cold politeness.

'This table, I think.' He led her to a table away from the others that was partially obscured from diners by a bank of potted plants, but with an unobstructed view of the river.

'So, if everything is okay, why did Mr Allonby come to try to headhunt me?' Other than Jarrod talking her up to the man at some point?

Dry cleaning. It could have been about dry cleaning.

'There are rumours circulating. They're widespread, very recent, and they've been placed for maximum effect to try and damage me financially.' The words were pushed through his teeth as his gaze bored into hers. 'Daniels's call was my first knowledge of this. He wanted to withdraw his portfolio from the company. I had a hard time convincing him to change his mind, despite refuting the rumours utterly.'

'So you're not in financial difficulty.' She nodded. That was as she'd expected. 'But someone wants you to be?'

'Apparently so.' His fist clenched on the table.

Who would do such a thing to him?

'Molly, things could get rough for a little while.' His gaze held hers as he uttered the words. 'Whoever started these rumours apparently has influence in the social circles I mix in.'

'And draw your business from.' Molly drew a deep breath. The glittery, glamorous, totally out-of-her-league world of Brisbane's highest society.

He dipped his head in acknowledgement. 'If more of those people become concerned about the safety of their investments—'

'You could lose accounts. Big accounts.' Anger and protectiveness welled from somewhere deep inside her. 'Who would do this to you? Why would anyone want to hurt your business? We have to put a stop to this!'

'I don't have business enemies.' He grimaced, shrugged his shoulders. 'Well, maybe I do. Apparently I have some kind of enemy out there. But I'm the one who makes more money for my clients. My dealings are fair and equitable, and I either work with people or I don't, depending on whether they choose to use me.'

His gaze roved to the river before it came back to rest on her face. As he stared at her, his expression hardened. 'I *will* put an end to this threat, you can rest assured of that.'

She believed him. And as her heart calmed her protectiveness became deep-seated determination. 'I'll do whatever I can to help you. We have two appointments for later this afternoon, with clients who wouldn't say why they wanted to come in. I wonder if they've heard the rumours?'

'It's probable, and probable they'll also want to pull their funds.' Their meals arrived and he fell silent. 'If I thought it would do any good, I'd phone some of my key social contacts and demand they reveal the source of the rumours. I will do that, as soon as we get back to the office, but I know it will be a waste of time.'

He jabbed his fork into his steak sandwich and carved off an end with his knife. 'There's a code about things like that, maybe because legal action is so easily entered into and can be so time-consuming and costly once it starts.'

'If your colleagues won't tell you who started the rumours, what will you do?' Molly picked a piece of walnut from her chicken Waldorf wrap and popped it into her mouth.

They ate in silence for a few minutes, and then the silence stretched and her skin began to prickle. She glanced up to find her boss's gaze fixed on her. He had a light of—something—in his eyes, and suddenly she felt uncomfortable, uncertain. Trapped in the beam of a pair of very determined eyes.

'Um…' Molly wrapped her A-line black skirt more firmly about her knees, and adjusted the green-and-black top though it needed no adjustment.

'It's imperative the company puts the strongest foot forward at this time. I want the person who started these rumours. I want the rumours stopped.' His face was a tight mask as he spoke the words. 'And I want any negative impact on my business not only fixed, but put so far behind in the face of my success no person would ever believe such a suggestion again.'

Well, she would have expected such strong assertions. In the three years she'd worked for him, he'd built his business from his own personal investments to a vibrant, diverse service on the cutting edge of financial investment for some very wealthy clients.

'You want a three-faceted approach to the problem.' She murmured the words as she thought it over. 'Catch the person who started the rumours and bring them to account for it. While working on that, fix any negative impact to the company. And, during that process, make us stronger than before so such a threat can't even touch us in the future.'

'That's it, and of course, after Allonby's offer to you, I also want people to understand you're staying with me.' He said this last in a low tone that brooked not even the thought of an argument—from anywhere. 'You'll be useful in any case, to help present a consolidated front.'

It was a simple desire to strengthen the company's position. The first part of his statement shouldn't have rushed across her senses. That it did was a problem, because it was one thing to have an intellectual admiration for his mind, even his personality, provided she kept that admiration work-related.

Anything else would be inappropriate, foolish. There couldn't be 'anything else'. And, yes, she'd had somewhat of a crush on her boss kind of from the beginning, actually, but that fact had to stay subjugated to the power of her will and common sense.

If occasionally she slipped, she understood the danger of it and quickly shored up her defences again.

Molly attempted to do so now. 'I'll be happy to put in extra hours in the office, make calls, send out letters. Whatever is needed to set these plans in action.'

'I do want extra hours from you.' He linked his fingers in front of him beside his plate.

He had beautiful hands, strong and lean, with a light dusting of hair across the backs.

Molly drew a deep breath and straightened her spine. Now was not the time to dwell on such things about her boss. Particularly when he was looking at her with such...

'I want those hours from you outside the office.' He dropped this statement on her without a blink. 'While we sort this out, I need you at my side for all my working time. We need to move fast and hard to get this thing sorted, one way or another. It's not about the money. I have enough that I could give up working right now and pay you to do the same. It's the principle of the thing. My business reputation.'

A reputation he'd formed among Brisbane's elite. Who were very much not people Molly had ever mixed with, or expected to mix with, other than to offer cups of tea or coffee when they arrived for an appointment at the office with her boss.

She doubted most of them would even be able to recall what she looked like, but it appeared her boss was asking her to...

'What do you mean, exactly?' She asked the question with a kind of forlorn hope, but she knew the answer. Until now she had worked in the office, and her boss had worked in the office, but he had also worked among his peers. He needed to have a presence in that world. In *his* world.

His world, but not hers. Mum, Izzy and Faye might have plied her with fairy tales during her childhood, might have told her she could have the sun, the stars and the moon with sugar on top if she liked, but reality was a whole other thing.

Their lives proved it. No money to speak of. No savings for the future whatsoever. Just a really expansive attitude towards treating themselves when they felt like it, which they justified was okay because they always made sure they could pay their bills on time. And when they no longer had jobs? Had reached retirement age and didn't have that income stream any more? What would happen then?

Molly pushed the thoughts away. She had enough to worry about at the moment!

It would be dangerous to spend extra time with Jarrod, not to mention she would be so utterly out of her depth. 'Mollyrella', in the glittery socialite world of money and privilege? Oh, no. Surely there was some other way? 'If you're suggesting I attend social outings with you, I don't think that would be a good idea.'

'It's the best idea.' He contradicted her with an implacable set to his jaw. 'That three-pronged plan has a better chance at success with both of us working on it. Two sets of eyes and ears, a dual approach to show them the company is strong and intact, employer and employee included.'

His argument made sense. Darn him. 'What about contacting your client base now to reassure them? Personal calls?'

'If I do that, it directly acknowledges the rumours, and

that may result in giving them further credence in their eyes.'
He shook his head. 'I want to see people's faces while we
search for the source of the rumours, while we talk up the
business in such a way that those who have concerns will
be reassured. Your statistical and other information recall
will help with that.'

He ate the last bite of his meal and pushed the plate away.
'This started in social circles. That's where it will have to be
resolved. It's as simple as that.'

'Simple' was not the word that came to Molly's mind.
Trapped, maybe. Trapped and outwitted and outmanoeuvred.
'Well, it's just—'

'We'll attend our first function tonight, a private art exhibition in the home and grounds of a couple I know.' He
named one of the wealthiest couples in the city. 'You'll come
as my guest.'

'I've heard of those people. They're almost as wealthy—'
As you and your parents. 'The function is just hours away from
now. I don't even own a suitable evening dress.'

I'm a hundred miles to not ready.

'I didn't realise you might not—' He broke off, blinked as
though to cover his reaction. 'Of course, I won't expect you to
be out of pocket while you help me, Molly. I'll reimburse any
costs. That means gowns, shoes, handbags—anything you need.'

No, no. That wasn't what she meant. Oh, how embarrassing,
and how great a reminder that they came from different worlds!
Who needed an evening gown to go to the movies with her
family, or out for a meal at a pizza place for a treat, after all?

'I appreciate your thoughtfulness,' she said stiffly. 'But
actually—'

'It's more than appropriate for you to have access to an
expense account to cover such costs while I'm asking these

extra duties of you.' His expression didn't change, yet somehow she sensed a softening in him. As though he understood this was awkward for her.

Or pitied her. If it was that, she'd toss herself into the river.

'My budget can stretch a little if need be.' It couldn't really, but her pride felt stretched thin enough already.

'I can't allow that.' As though he sensed her ongoing resistance and was determined to roll right over it, he went on. 'You can shop for a dress this afternoon. I'll give you one of my account cards. This is simply business, Molly. I want you properly equipped to function in this new role, that's all. For that reason, you'll accept assistance with such purchases because they're legitimate work-related expenses.

'If it's any consolation, I'm not thrilled about this turn of events.' He grimaced. 'I'd rather spend the weekend at my cottage by the sea, putting the finishing touches to my yacht, but nobody messes with my business and gets away with it.'

'You-you're almost finished building your yacht?' He'd shown her the schematics months ago. In a rare moment she had treasured, they'd put their heads together over his desk and had got quite excited, until Molly had remembered her place and straightened. 'Are you happy with the results?' She snapped her teeth together before any more questions could emerge. She was avoiding the real issue, anyway.

'The yacht is almost done and I'm looking forward to sailing it.' As though he knew her tactics perfectly, he turned the attention back to their previous discussion. 'You'll also be paid overtime for the extra hours you work. Double for out-of-office hours, triple on Sundays. Don't argue about it. The decision is made.'

'Sundays, plural?' She didn't want to be out of her comfort zone too long, but his solid approach to not only resolving the current problem but also protecting against a repeat, yes, that all would take time.

Molly suppressed another updraft of panic. She would have to find a way to ease out of things after the initial strike. Surely that would be possible?

'Whatever it takes. The art exhibition will be a start.' He drew a breath. 'But, realistically, only a start. Even if we are able to track down the rumourmonger immediately, there's still damage control and shoring up to be done.'

'How many events are we talking about? How much, ah, out of hours time I guess is what I mean? A night or two per week, or—?'

'A full onslaught at first. There's the art exhibition tonight, and then a charity auction tomorrow, Saturday. That won't be quite as formal.' He paused to think. 'There'll be more. I'll need to check my calendar to see what else is happening.'

Two events; two to worry about for now. She simply wouldn't think beyond those two until she had to. Molly drew a breath and told herself that wasn't so bad.

She would do the job asked of her, be eyes and ears and a show of strength, and be back at her desk Monday morning in PA mode, contained and unscathed as ever.

She wouldn't embarrass him, and she wouldn't fall prey to other feelings about him either just because they would be seeing each other away from their desks.

See? All sorted.

Except for her unease about spending his money. And a few dozen other worries all seething away in there. 'I can provide my own clothes for the second event. Things I already have.'

'If you wish, but be prepared to purchase a number of evening dresses at my cost.' He rose from the table, drew out his wallet and handed her a card from within. Even the gold colouring of the plastic looked expensive. 'You'll use this for purchases.'

When he lowered his head to murmur the code to operate the card, Molly stood very still and forced her mind to think of those numbers, not his closeness. She almost succeeded.

'We'll head back. I'll make those key phone-calls while you shop.' He gestured for her to precede him from the outdoor area.

They left the restaurant and began to retrace their earlier steps.

'When I get back to the office I'll create a spreadsheet of the names of all our clients so we can keep track of who we've talked to. I'll take the PDA with me tonight.' Molly dived into plans and strategies, workaday ones—because those were safe, normal and about the truth of their relationship, even if Jarrod's decisions had shaken the edges of that truth for her today.

At least he hadn't offered to help her shop. That would have been *too* unnerving!

CHAPTER TWO

'ACTUALLY, the spreadsheet will require a list of clients *and* associates. We'll want to track all the significant people we've talked to, or am I going too far with the tracking idea?' All the significant wealthy, upper-class, socialite so-far-out-of-her-reach people. Molly's mouth flattened.

'That will be fine. We can sort out a list of names this afternoon.' Jarrod touched her elbow again to guide her along the street.

The Prince led Cinderella along the streets of Brisbane so she could go and buy a pretty dress.

Cinderella stared at him through her geeky glasses, while tingles tiptoed up her arm and scurried down her spine simply because of a touch.

Molly suppressed a snort. Cinderella indeed. Her mum, Aunt Izzy and Faye might think like that, might dream pie-in-the-sky dreams with no foundation in reality. Molly knew better, and she *would* stick to that knowledge. Heck, just the thought of being in his world made her knees want to knock together. She should focus on that!

'You'll have a chance to use that latest software package and the PDA uplink.' Jarrod had insisted she purchase the software when he'd noticed she had it circled in a catalogue.

'That way, if you take electronic notes over the weekend, the data collation will be as streamlined as possible afterwards.'

'Yes, it will.' Molly fell silent.

They were a block away from the building that housed their suite of offices when a voice spoke from behind them.

'Jarrod.' The tone was cultured, deep and rather devoid of expression.

Her boss's body seemed to tighten. In fact, he seemed to tighten all over—posture, expression, muscle and sinew. Prickly. Wary. Was it because of the rumours? Was this someone from his world?

Molly's gaze sought his, but he'd already clasped her elbow. He turned her until they faced a well-dressed middle-aged couple. 'Dad, Mum. What brings you to this part of the city?'

His parents! Molly had never met them. They didn't come to her boss's office. He didn't talk about them. She had assumed he didn't feel his personal life was any of her business.

'You're right to be surprised by our presence here.' Jarrod's mother spoke the words through chilly lips. 'We usually delegate such tasks as shopping, but sometimes they are unavoidable.'

'We won't be here long. Just taking care of one essential matter,' Jarrod's father added.

'I rather enjoy the shopping experience.' Jarrod made the observation in a mild tone, but there were shutters down over his face.

For some reason Molly couldn't help edging closer to her boss's side.

'We're here on business.' His mother made the announcement as though it meant everything. 'We're to be guests of the king of an island country.'

She named the country, a small but beautiful paradise

Molly had only read about and seen in travel documentaries, and went on.

'We came to collect a gift we've had handcrafted. The king may agree to import our Road Ten furnishings into the country. It's necessary to impress him.'

'Good luck with that.' Jarrod said it amenably enough. When Molly shifted slightly at his side, he forced a smile to his face. 'We've been remiss in the introductions. This is my personal assistant, Molly Taylor. Molly, my parents, Stuart and Elspeth Banning.'

'Hello.' Molly offered her best professional smile.

Jarrod's father dipped his head infinitesimally. His mother didn't even bother with that.

When his parents all but snubbed his PA, a growl came out of Jarrod's throat before he could stop it.

He would tolerate his parents' coldness towards him. Hell, that had been his lot since the day he'd been born. But they could be polite to Molly, and if not...

'Perhaps I should walk on ahead, leave you to say your hellos.' Molly's pointy chin went up. Strands of brown hair had escaped her ponytail and blew softly against her neck and cheek in the mild, warm breeze. She chased them with her fingertips.

A girl in clunky shoes and an odd, wraparound top and A-line skirt. He hadn't liked hearing Allonby's offer to her. He didn't like his parents staring through her either. 'No need, Molly. We're done here.'

He turned to his parents one last time. 'You'll excuse us. Enjoy your time out of the country.'

Before Molly could more than blink, he hustled her away. He'd wondered if his parents had heard the rumours. He might have asked, but somehow he doubted they'd have remained silent on the topic if they knew something. They'd probably been out of the country too much recently to hear anything.

If they *did* hear something, and dared to raise the topic with him, he would soon set them straight that his business was fine.

He and Molly reached the outside of their office building. He came to a halt. 'Time for you to get that dress.'

'Yes.' She clutched her handbag in her fingers.

Was she worried she might lose the contents? Or lose his account card?

'When I return I'll get straight to work on the spreadsheet.' She hurried off into the crowd.

Jarrod stepped into the building, returned to their office suite and made the obligatory phone calls. They netted exactly the results he had expected—namely none.

It galled him to feel his business was even slightly at the mercy of someone's whispered words. The sooner he and Molly got out there amongst it to set things to rights, the happier he would be. He would talk up business, while Molly spouted facts and figures and information she stored in vast quantities in that geek-girl head of hers.

On these thoughts, Jarrod immersed himself in investment strategy. If once or twice he paused to wonder how long Molly would be, or what her dress would look like, he quickly pushed the thoughts aside.

'I'm back.' Molly spoke the unnecessary words in a sudden fit of nerves as she reentered her office space almost an hour after leaving Jarrod outside the building. She wished she could ask about his parents, about that chilly meeting earlier, but she doubted Jarrod would welcome any questions.

Maybe the couple warmed up when they weren't in public.

'I tried not to take too much time. How did the phone calls go? And has anyone else phoned for appointments or anything?'

He sat behind his desk, an array of printed reports spread before him as he clicked through various screens on his computer. At her words he got to his feet and strode towards her. 'The phone calls went predictably. No one would reveal anything. There have been no other requests for appointments. You got all you needed?'

His gaze shifted to the bag in her hands, and Molly wished she hadn't spoken at all. She wanted to forget about tonight until she absolutely had to face it. Maybe by then her nerves would be under control and her defences back in place, as she needed them to be.

What if the event was really swanky and she did or said something stupid—stepped on the hem of someone's designer gown and ripped it right off, like you saw in the movies?

'Perhaps there won't be any more damage from the rumours, and, yes, I got a dress.' And at a reasonable price that wouldn't make her cringe too much to know he'd paid for it. 'Right. Well, the first client isn't due for fifteen minutes, and I'd best study that phone-system so it can't spring any more surprises on either of us.'

They'd had enough of accidental eavesdropping for the day. 'But I'll do it quickly and then get onto the spreadsheet, unless you have other instructions for me?' She hovered beside the desk and wished he would go back to his.

'No other instructions for now.' Jarrod gestured to the bag in her hand. 'Would you like to hang up your purchase? I have spare hangers in my dressing-room closet.'

'No!' She tried to pull herself together. 'I mean, no thanks. The dress looks quite crushproof, and, if it isn't, I'll iron it tonight.'

She didn't want to go into the inner sanctum of Jarrod's dressing room. That would require her to walk through his gym room and past his bathroom, which she had avoided doing for the past three years.

Her boss often came to work early, exercised and showered and dressed right here. Molly knew this from the office's alarm time-records, and because she had glimpsed the rooms now and then when he had his rear-office door open. She didn't want to get any closer or more knowledgeable, didn't want to visualise him working out, or under that spray of water.

She had enough trouble to deal with! 'I have to get moving. There's a lot to do this afternoon. Seventy-two pages of PDF manual, the spreadsheet, your appointments, plus any other work you want me to do.'

'And despite today's disruptions I have investments to manage, which will result in that handing off in about—' he glanced at the clock on the wall '—an hour from now, if I can have my first appointment back out the door in half that time.

'Good work, Molly. The dress, I mean.' He turned, walked the few paces to his office and stepped inside. 'For the rest, I'll find a way to make up for losing Daniels's business. I won't allow these rumours to win out over me.'

'I know you won't. I'll get to work.' Molly stuffed the bag into her drawer, drew a shaky breath and brought up the phone-manual file on her computer and started to read it.

The first appointment came and went. The client didn't withdraw her business, but Jarrod's jaw was tight when Molly made coffee and took it in to him. Appointment number two was worse. The elderly man had made up his mind before he even came through the door. He was out again five minutes later, and Molly knew they'd lost him.

Two more phone calls came in requesting urgent appointments, and they had a walk-in as well whom Jarrod saw immediately.

When the last appointment finally left for the day, Molly had five minutes to go if she wanted to catch her bus. She made her way to Jarrod's office and stood just inside the door.

He sat strong and straight behind his desk as always. It was only because she knew him so well that she could see the tension beneath the surface.

'How bad—?'

'Eight million short-term investment dollars gone, spread across three different clients. Mrs Armiga is sitting on the fence on the issue for now. I successfully reassured the other client.' His eyes closed briefly in a small sign of weariness he wouldn't have wanted her to notice. 'If the clients who withdrew their short-term monies had been able, they'd have taken the rest of their funds today as well.'

The clients had signed investment agreements. 'They have to honour the arrangements they've made with you.'

He shook his head. 'True in theory, but, with the alternative that they would immediately start legal proceedings to get the funds released, I agreed to transfer control to them. That will be done on Monday.'

Molly's mouth tightened and angry words burst out. 'I hope their investments do badly. I hope they buy stocks and bonds that sink without a trace. I hope their favourite underwear gets washed with a colour-leaky red shirt that's covered in fluff and has paper in the pockets!'

'I'll recoup the losses, Molly.' His low words were warm, calming, a little amused in a grim kind of way—*encouraged* as well as encouraging?

Jarrod gestured her closer to his desk. 'I know we've run

over time. Give me your address details. We need to be at the venue tonight at seven p.m.' He explained the general location.

She nodded, remembered the whole 'Mollyrella goes into society' thing, and her stomach knotted afresh. Well, she couldn't pull out, could she? Eight million dollars gone already, more on the way.

The three-faceted attack plan needed to be put into action just as much as Jarrod had intimated. 'The trip should take about half an hour from my flat.'

'I'll call for you at six-thirty. Can you be ready in time? If not, I can drive you home now as well.'

He'd never done that, had never offered, or needed to.

'I could take a taxi both ways tonight.' Would it cost a lot? Probably. 'And I can make the bus on time now.' She shifted in the chair on the other side of his desk and tried not to notice how good he looked backlit by the city's skyscape— tall buildings, cloudless sky. Battle-sharp hazel eyes watched her so intently.

'No taxi. I want to brief you further on the way there.'

Right. 'I'll just jot down my address, then. It's on file, but this will be quicker for you.'

And babble out the ridiculous while she was at it. Molly bit her lip, and reached for his sticky notepad and a pen. As she handed the address over, she asked one last question. 'Do you think Mrs Armiga will come round?'

'I don't know. She listened to what I had to say, and then said she's always thought I looked too smooth.' He got to his feet in a sharp movement. 'What does she mean by that? Well, the outcome is our client is not convinced she can trust me, but she hasn't pulled her file—yet, at least.'

I'd say you're more whisky-smooth: delicious, but with a kick.

She hadn't said that aloud, had she? No, of course not.

Get a grip, Molly!

'Tonight we'll start to turn the tide back our way. You've got some great cutting-edge strategies you've implemented even in the last month.' Molly headed for her office, drew out her handbag and the carrier bag. 'We'll talk the business up, and people will begin to realise the rumours can't be true.'

Jarrod followed behind her. 'Don't be worried for me, Molly, will you? I'm annoyed as hell, and I won't stop until this situation is completely resolved, but it *will* be.'

'I know. I have complete faith in you.' Not so much in herself, but she'd committed to this now and she wouldn't turn back. Not while he needed her.

He paused with his hand on the light switch, and for a moment his brows drew down and his gaze flared as he stared at her. Then he shook his head, flicked the switch, and they stepped out.

They got into the lift. Molly breathed in and out and commanded herself to *calm down*. That look… Well, it had just been a look, right?

She was all out of sorts. It was the dress, and the stress, and spending his money on herself, and having to dive into that social world, all together. Belly flop, more like.

'You're not too smooth.' She spoke the words to fill the silence, and then attempted to explain. 'I don't mean you're not smooth personally. I'm sure you're as smooth as is appropriate, and that's none of my concern, anyway. But, in business, you're exactly the right amount of non-smooth.'

'Thank you.' Did his lips twitch before he turned away? 'I appreciate that explanation.'

Molly faced forward and wished they'd get to street level. When they finally did, she scooted off the lift so fast she almost didn't fit through the gap in the still-opening doors.

'I'll be ready at six-thirty.' She would completely get over this feeling of impending panic between now and then, take control of herself and be ready to present an utterly business-like front when he called to collect her.

Yes. That was much better. 'I've got the work PDA with me. I'll bring it as we agreed, so I can keep track of names and information. Goodbye.' Molly bolted and didn't look back, even if she was a little tempted.

She half-jogged her way to the bus stop and tried not to feel uptight about the upcoming events. With a PDA in her hand and a clear agenda, this didn't have to feel all that different from a day in the office.

And what if it took a week, or two weeks, or a month, or three months, before she could safely draw back? All that time at her boss's side—days, weekends, evenings—to make it really hard to remember he was her boss and she was his PA, and nothing else could possibly be…

Nonsense.

Nonsense, the idea of them being anything else to each other, and to this taking three months. The rumour issue would be resolved fast and that was that!

In celebration of this utter certainty, that was no certainty at all but what she so wanted to believe, Molly slumped into a seat on the bus, drew her phone from her bag and sent a text message to her mother.

Do you think Faye would have a pair of sandals I could wear with a burgundy evening-dress? I have to go out on business with my boss tonight.

There. See? All about business. A few moments later Molly opened her mum's return message.

I checked with Faye. She has a pair of sandals with glass beading all over them. Three-inch heel. They'd go with anything. How exciting, Molly. A chance to do something grand for the night!

Yeah. Great. And glass-beaded sandals with a no-doubt uncomfortable heel would do nicely. The pumpkin coach could drop her and her broken toes off at her flat at midnight.

The phone rang in her hand. Molly jumped, and then answered. 'I don't know about glass-beaded sandals, Mum. Maybe something a bit more sensible would be better. Personally I don't see why people don't just stick to shoes with a thick strap and a decent tread, like I do for work and weekends.'

A long pause of silence ensued and she realised she might have sounded a bit ungrateful. Molly drew a breath. 'Mum?'

'I take it you made your bus on time?' Her boss's voice poured into her ear.

And he was definitely smiling this time. She didn't need to see him to know it.

'Yes. Yes, I did make the bus on time.' Molly sat up straighter in her seat, not that he could see her. Jarrod had her number for emergencies. She'd put it into his mobile phone herself. Why hadn't she checked the display before answering? He had never called before, and she'd made a right goose of herself, hadn't she, blathering on about shoes?

In the background she heard a clattering sound—the underground roller-door of their building going up?

Molly pictured him driving his car one-handed, mobile phone in the other. 'You're not allowed to drive and talk on your mobile phone. You could have an accident.' Great. Now she sounded like a mother hen.

'I know. We bought Bluetooth, remember?' *Oh, yes.* He definitely sounded amused.

Enough to make her hopes of regaining control of her changed circumstances, of riding it out with barely a ripple in the usual fabric of her work for him, threaten to crumble. Things were changing already, and she hadn't even sorted out her shoes.

He went on. 'The phone is on hands-free. I always use the technology we buy.'

'Oh. Good, then.' It was silly to feel so gratified by his words. No, her heart simply stuttered in *shock* that she had forgotten about the purchase even for a moment. In her defence, she'd had a long and trying day, and it wasn't over yet.

'I wanted to tell you to eat something before tonight.' His voice returned to a more usual tone. 'It's only drinks and nibbles, and I don't want you to be hungry.'

'Thank you. That was thoughtful.' If Molly knew her family, either Faye or Izzy or both would be ready for her when she arrived at the group of three flats they rented. They would have sandwiches in hand, and be ready to throw open their wardrobes so she could pick a pair of shoes and any other accessories she might deem necessary for the evening.

And her mother would be waiting to hear about it by phone as she went about her evening cleaning-job in a building full of offices not so different from the one Molly had just left.

Generous. They were generous...to a fault.

'I'll be sure to eat.' If she could push anything down over the knot of unease currently lodged halfway up her oesophagus.

'Then I'll see you soon. We'll take care of this, Molly. Between us, we'll do it.'

'I'll do my best to help you.' Not to embarrass him in front of his peers. Not to embarrass herself. Molly's tummy contorted into fifty different balloon-shaped animals, and stayed bunched in all those multicoloured knots.

'See you soon.' Jarrod ended the call.

Molly put her phone away and peeked into the bag at her hastily purchased dress. So there would be an art exhibition.

She'd attended some free ones at Turbine Hall and other places. No difference, really—other than the whole glitterati, buckets of money; nothing like her lifestyle.

And so her boss had phoned when he never had before. Things had changed; she had to expect he might ring, or whatever. They both needed to adapt. Molly simply needed to control her responses to him as she had always done, no matter the surroundings or circumstances at the time, and everything would be fine.

Izzy and Faye went one better than throwing open their wardrobes. They were waiting on her doorstep, arms full of all sorts of offerings, sandwiches included. Well, they did only have to walk from the flats either side of Molly's to be there. Guilt rose in Molly's chest, because they were wonderful, and giving, and always had been, and she shouldn't resent them...

Where had that thought come from? The two women started to talk at once, and Molly ushered them inside.

At six twenty-five, Izzy leaned close to adjust the necklace around Molly's neck for about the fifth time.

'You look beautiful, Molly.' Strands of frizzled red hair brushed Molly's face as her aunt hugged her. 'I'm so glad you chose to wear this pendant. It really suits the dress.'

A fine gold chain held a large Broome pearl in the shape of a squished piece of confectionery. Izzy had bought it two years ago with a work bonus from the courier company that employed her. Money she could have socked away into savings. Her pleasure now in lending the thing made Molly's tummy knot all over again.

Faye stepped closer and glanced at Molly's feet. 'It's worth a whole week of selling electric frying-pans over the phone just to see you in those lovely shoes. I always mean to wear them when I buy them.'

'There are worse things than a shoe addiction.' The pronouncement came over the speakerphone into Molly's small living room.

Her mum's voice, and Molly knew what would be next, because she'd heard it before.

Faye leaned close to the phone. 'You don't buy all that much Swiss chocolate and French perfume, Anna, and it's only when you actually import it that it really costs.'

'Don't get caught on the phone when you should be cleaning, Mum. You're not at someone's desk, are you?' Until a year ago, Molly and her mum had shared a rented flat two suburbs away, but the one-bedroom flat between Izzy and Faye's had become available. It was closer to Molly's work, and they'd all insisted Molly should move into it, that it was time she had her own place.

Anna had taken in a weekday boarder, and Molly's fate had been sealed. She did enjoy having her own space and being closer to her work, but...

'I'm perfectly safe, Molly.' Her mother's voice was calm and unruffled. 'Local phone calls to close relatives are permitted from the tearoom. I'm treating this as my break time.'

Molly relaxed. That was okay, then.

'He's here!' Izzy made this announcement from her position at the curtained lounge window. Her words pulled Molly's mind from family worries to work ones.

'Molly. He's gorgeous.' Izzy twitched the edge of the curtain back into place and turned to glance at her. 'Why didn't you ever say?'

'I didn't notice.' *Liar.* 'He's my boss. I don't see him that way.' *Great big liar.*

Now he was here, and the two of them were about to go out, would it be okay? Molly's heart rolled over and played dead. Just like her dog, Horse, in one of his silly moods when he wanted her to pet him and rub his tummy and tell him what a good boy he was. On cue, a foghorn woof sounded from the flats' communal back yard.

Molly forced breath back into her lungs, and used it to once again try to explain things. 'This is business. It's not a date. It's nothing to get excited about.'

'If you say so.' Faye tiptoed to the phone and picked it up, whispered something Molly couldn't hear, and hung up. Then she tiptoed towards the back door of Molly's flat. 'We'll just leave quietly. You look like a million dollars, anyway, you really do. Whether you want to treat it as a date or not.'

'You look like a princess.' Izzy followed Faye, also on tiptoes. 'Maybe you'll meet someone there who'll sweep you off your feet, if not your boss.'

Fairy tales again. There'd never been any telling them. Both women slipped out the door. Molly locked it behind them. She didn't want to meet anyone. The only feelings she had…

Were completely controllable. Molly went to her room to collect her bag—also borrowed. She felt the comforting weight of the PDA in there, and drew a breath aimed at steadying her nerves.

There were footsteps on the path outside, on the porch, and then the doorbell chimed.

'Coming,' Molly muttered. *Coming, ready or not.*

CHAPTER THREE

JARROD waited on the porch of Molly's tiny flat. The flats on either side sported cluttered yards full of potted plants, garden gnomes and odd bits of small statuary. Molly's yard had a miniature rose-bush either side of the path near the porch, a neat little area of lawn and nothing else.

The area didn't tell him much about his PA's private life, not that he needed to know.

Jarrod smoothed his hand over his tie and acknowledged he felt tense, keyed up. Understandable. His business was under attack and he wanted that fixed.

Footsteps sounded inside Molly's apartment, the tap of heels on parquet.

His PA had made that odd comment about shoes when she'd answered her phone, so maybe it only sounded like heels. Even so, he wondered briefly how she would be dressed. In classic black, maybe, something that covered her from neck to toe and went with her thick-framed glasses. Before he finished the thought, the door swung open.

Molly stood on the other side, but it wasn't the Molly he knew and worked with. It was a vision of a woman with silky dark hair flowing about her shoulders, a flawless face, big brown eyes, and her perfect figure outlined in a beautifully simple burgundy dress that left her arms bare, outlined her curves, dipped in at her waist and flared all the way to her feet.

'I'm ready. I have the PDA. Izzy and Faye made sandwiches and I talked them out of three layers of necklaces and fifteen cheapskate arm-bracelets.' The words tumbled breathlessly over each other, and his PA's face flushed in a way that made her look even more becoming. 'That is, I'm ready to leave.'

'I'm glad you're ready,' he said rather stupidly. Was his jaw hanging open? He clenched his teeth, just to make sure that wasn't the case.

'Yes,' she muttered through softly parted lips. 'I'm ready to beard the vultures—that is, to *see the sculptures.*'

'You're wearing heels.' This was said rather accusingly. He tried to soften his tone. 'You don't—at work.'

The sandals on her feet did indeed have heels. They were also encrusted in small glass beads, and he couldn't seem to take his gaze from toenails painted with burgundy polish to match that on her short, trimmed fingernails. He forced his gaze slowly back up, and noticed the delicate pearl necklace that lay in the valley between her breasts.

'Not—I don't usually, no.' She lowered her hand from the doorknob.

He couldn't remember what they'd been talking about so he made the only announcement that came to mind. 'We should go.'

His voice sounded about an octave lower than usual. His ears buzzed, and he couldn't seem to catch his breath. A wash of warmth flooded his bloodstream as he added, 'You're also not wearing your glasses.'

Brilliant conversation, Banning. Any chance you can do better before she decides you're a complete, dithering fool?

He cleared his throat. 'You look very nice, though— glasses or not.'

Far more than that. Sweet, desirable, hot…

A tight feeling caught at his chest. He thought it might be panic—because this was like seeing her for the first time, and he felt as though he'd missed something that was right there. And how could he have missed it for so long? Worse, why did the sight of her this way have such a strong impact on him? He, who felt so little, whose family had bred that lack of feeling into his DNA with their coldness and their lack of love or any kind of gentle feeling?

It must simply be sexual awareness, though that had never jolted him in quite this intense, unexpected way. The thought didn't exactly help, given it was inappropriate all by itself. Heat warmed the back of his neck as he tried to batten down his reaction to her. Molly was his assistant. This was a working night. The clothes, the appearance, might be different, but nothing had changed between them.

Nothing other than that his eyes had been opened to her.

Well, he could just close them again, couldn't he?

Molly stepped out onto the porch and pulled the door forward until the lock clicked into place. Her gaze skittered over his charcoal suit-coat, the grey shirt and darker grey silk tie, down to his feet and up again. 'I like—I like—um, your tie. It matches the colour in your eyes. Yes. You look nice, too. You do. Of course.'

She looked away. 'That is, the tie matches one of the colours in your eyes, but at the moment they're mostly grey, not so much on the hazel side of things.'

'I didn't think my eyes changed colours much.' He'd never noticed.

'Oh, they do. I mean, it appears they have. At the moment—' She stopped the words.

There'd been something in her eyes for just a moment.

Interest—reluctant, unexpected perhaps, as his had been—but there.

He didn't want that. Didn't want to think of her that way, or her to think that way of him; he didn't want this to be personal at all. Such reactions could only cause trouble. So why did the knowledge that she'd studied him closely enough to notice nuances of his eyes almost please him?

'Right. You're ready to leave, to get to work on this problem that's been tossed at the business?' Perhaps if he repeated the words aloud he would remember the purpose of this night, and get his mind off the vision Molly made in the eyeball-searing dress.

'Yes. I'm keen to start sorting this matter out.' She dropped her key into a small clutch-bag made of some kind of shimmery cloth. Her tone was all business, but her hand shook as she carried out the small, ordinary act.

Jarrod searched her gaze, and something passed between them that heated his skin a second time.

His hand lifted towards her face before he registered the desire to touch. He dropped it away again, turned aside. 'Then let's go search for a rumourmonger, spread subtle reassurance and build up the business with as many people as we can along the way.'

'Yes. Let's.' Molly nodded a little too vehemently.

And Jarrod told himself to relax. This was just work, after all.

Molly's tummy danced an out-of-control jig as she settled into the car beside Jarrod. The sedan was midnight-blue, and the engine gave a muscled purr when her boss turned the key in the ignition.

She wanted to blame her tummy flutters solely on nerves about the upcoming evening. That accounted for part of it, but there was more. The look in his eyes just now. Surely she had misinterpreted that, *imagined* that altogether?

'I've never seen you without your glasses before.'

He murmured the words as he steered the sleek sedan through the city streets.

It was an observation about her person, and it wouldn't have occurred a day ago. It was *change*, and in this instance Molly wanted to be as immovable as the most stubborn non-embracer of change.

'I wear contacts occasionally.' She almost said 'on special occasions'—but this wasn't one. Instead, she took the PDA from her purse and cast a repressive glance his way that was equally aimed at herself. 'Glasses are far more sensible, in my opinion, even if Izzy and Faye—'

Molly cut herself off. Her boss didn't need to hear about that. Work. What she needed was work. 'There wasn't time this afternoon to get the names of the people you hope to speak with tonight who aren't our clients. If you can tell me now, I'll key them into the organiser for reference later. Also, now you've had a little time to consider it, can you think of *anyone* who might want to do this to you?'

'I have a couple of old school rivals, but I don't have any true leads on this.' His frustration showed through as his hands tightened on the steering wheel. 'Either people are my clients, in which case I look after them, or they're not, and what I do with my work is irrelevant to them.'

'Maybe a thwarted girlfriend might be behind the rumours?'

The moment she said the words, Molly wished them unsaid. So much for keeping to business, because that subject was so *not* her business! Besides, in the time Molly had known him, Jarrod had shown no signs of any significant relationship. He seemed to prefer to date casually and sporadically.

Without commitment. His parents' coldness this afternoon came back to her. He could be aloof, sure, and maybe it was odd that he hadn't been in any deep relationships since she'd known him—but lots of people just weren't ready.

She chose not to remember that *her* last date had practically been aeons ago. 'Never mind about that. It's probably more important to get that list of key names together.'

'Yes, quite, and there's been no one of significance, in any case. I don't do the commitment thing.' He started tossing out names of associates.

Molly wondered about those words, but he didn't give her time to dwell on them. She duly made notes about his associates.

After a time, Jarrod turned his car through a set of gates. 'This is the Laurant family's estate.' He stopped at the signal of a gloved attendant. 'The car will be parked for us. Wait there. I'll come round for you.'

Molly drew a sharp breath. Other thoughts receded as she stared at the grounds and mansion. People strolled across vast lawns and along bordered walkways. Glittery, wealthy people like her boss—whether she tried not to think about that side of him during office hours or not.

And here was Molly—working class to the tips of her cheaply painted toenails. They were being valet-parked, for heaven's sake, whereas she didn't even own a car.

Jarrod opened her door. 'Ready?'

'Not exactly.' But she pasted a smile on her face and climbed out.

The first group of people Jarrod led her to comprised a woman somewhere between forty and fifty, a man with white hair and a trimmed moustache of the same tone and two women a few years older than Molly's own twenty-three years.

They were all dressed immaculately, with jewels dripping

from ears, wrists and necks, and they were critiquing a sculpture mounted on a platform at a curve in the crushed-granite pathway.

'The lines, darling. Look at that form and grace.'

'And wrought-iron for those edges. Such an intriguing choice.'

Molly glanced at the sculpture, and then stared. She couldn't help it. It was beautiful. Better than anything she had seen.

A combination of swirls, arcs and dips gave a sense of movement so real, she reached out to clutch Jarrod's arm, and a gush of awe came out of her. 'It's lovely. Like the sea swirling around rocks on a clear warm day. It's such a privilege to get to see something like this.'

Four heads turned towards them. Four sets of eyes stared askance at her.

Blurt city; great way to start the night.

Molly went to drop her hand away from her boss as unobtrusively as possible, but he tucked it through his crooked elbow and covered it with his other hand.

'Good evening.' Jarrod stepped forward, his tone urbane, calm. As though her gauche observations hadn't happened.

The Prince rescued Cinderella from her case of foot-in-mouth disease and probably wished he'd never brought her along.

'Allow me to introduce Molly Taylor.' His fingers squeezed over hers briefly before he dropped his hand—but he didn't release her from that elbow tuck. 'Molly is my PA, and right hand to me at Banning Financial Services.'

Correct. And she had a job to do for him tonight and couldn't afford to mess it up. 'Hello. It's a lovely evening, isn't it?' Molly tried to sound as though she did this kind of thing all the time.

The man smiled a little. She wasn't sure quite what he was thinking. The women didn't.

Jarrod introduced each person by name. For the next few minutes her boss discussed a variety of generalities. It was all about subtle probing, assertion of his confident stance, assurances given and offers made without a direct word being spoken.

Molly listened, and watched and waited for her turn. She didn't have a lot to say about the cost of importing ancient jade artefacts from a private dealer in Asia, which was where the conversation had drifted at the moment.

'My Aunt Izzy works at a courier's office' didn't seem quite appropriate, nor did describing her own brief stint after high school in a company that sold fertiliser, nor any of her other jobs before she'd landed the one with Jarrod.

When the conversation turned to her boss's work more directly at last, she tried not to sag with relief. He discussed some of his hottest recent investment efforts. Molly inserted statistical facts and figures where appropriate.

This she could do, and his bent head and, 'Good work, Molly,' whispered against her ear helped allay some of her unease. For a moment, at least, though that brush of his breath made it hard to think!

Her boss released her arm, only to lay a hand against her back between her shoulder blades. Though she knew he did it as an act of solidarity, and perhaps to silently commend her contribution to the conversation, her skin burned beneath his touch. She forced herself to stand still, to focus. And couldn't see any hint as to whether these people had heard rumours. The highly polished social veneer was just too blinding for her to tell.

Jarrod wound things up at just the right moment. 'The thing is to keep sharp. I'm sure the world of finance will change many times before I hit retirement age, for example— if I decide to give up my work even then.'

That was his statement: *I'm here to stay.*

'I might give you a call.' The man he had introduced as Phillip Yates smiled through his moustache. 'Must admit, I'd wondered how things were going, but I can see— Well, a fellow can never have too much good advice about investment, and what you've just said backs up everything I've heard about the best side of it. Interesting statistics, too.'

That was quite positive! Molly made a mental note to put those results in the PDA. She caught herself smiling a little, and caught a snide glance from one of the women as a sharp gaze raked over her clothing and back up again.

Molly's smile faded, though she told herself to buck up. She didn't belong here, with them in their designer originals and her in her modest dress and borrowed shoes and bag. She could have spent Jarrod's money on something very expensive, either, and they'd still have seen she was a fraud. It didn't matter what people thought of her, provided she and Jarrod achieved their goals.

Molly's fingers tightened involuntarily around Jarrod's arm and he glanced down at her. Smiled. Patted her hand.

'Give Molly a call at work. She'll sort out an appointment for you.' With that he propelled her away from the group.

Molly hauled out the PDA and started to key as though her life depended on it.

Jarrod let her for just a few moments, and then he drew her into a quiet nook beneath an enormous fig tree.

'What's the matter? I thought you paled just now. Are you unwell?'

'No. No, I'm fine.' She tipped up her chin. 'Can we keep going? I want us to cover as much ground as possible tonight.'

He frowned and seemed about to press the matter, but she tugged at his arm and he gave in, for the moment, at least.

They moved on, and got back into the thick of things. Molly watched her P's and Q's with everyone and tried not to dwell on her awareness of her boss. Tried to remember she really didn't belong here. Yet every time she told herself this her boss would cast a glance her way, or his hand would linger that little bit longer than necessary at her back, and finally she admitted it to herself.

Maybe it was only the dress—*no doubt* it was only the dress—but Jarrod was noticing her tonight. As a man noticed a woman. And, the more she thought about that, the more her heart thundered with all sorts of wild and nefarious thoughts. *Dream on.* Mum and the others would be proud, which should be enough to stop her thoughts right there.

'Champagne, wine or juice?' Jarrod's words broke through her reverie.

A drink waiter stood before them, tray held deftly aloft. Molly stared at the beverages. Juice might be the smartest choice. 'Champagne, please,' she blurted, because she'd never had it, and why not? And it would only be one glass.

'I'll have a Chardonnay.' Jarrod took their drinks and handed Molly's to her.

She had the good sense at least not to get the bubbles up her nose.

They visited one group after another for the next three hours. Jarrod nursed his wine.

Molly somehow ended up with a second glass of champagne, but that was okay, as it helped settle her nerves. She wasn't doing too badly at all, really.

'There's a display of smaller works in the ballroom of the house.' Jarrod leaned down to speak the words near her ear as they headed in that direction. 'We've covered about two thirds of our client base, plus some others. We'll speak to what people we can inside. You're not tired, Molly? Your feet aren't sore from all the standing about?'

Her ear tingled. She drew a breath that was too short and sharp, and took care to ease it out again unobtrusively. As for the shoes? 'The sandals fit as though they were made for me. I haven't felt a pinch or a painful twinge all night.' She frowned.

'I'm glad to hear that.' He sounded confused.

No doubt because her observation had come out with a 'don't start that glass-beaded stuff with me again' warning to herself embedded in it.

This was *work*, and she had to see it out, even if so far they had no lead on the source of the rumours.

They did their tour inside. Talked the talk, looked over the smaller sculptures on display. Got into a heated debate with each other about Biomemesis and Jon Denaro's— another artist's—take on biological death and the fear of the ocean's depths.

Molly drove home a particularly irrefutable belief on the topic by jabbing her finger against Jarrod's chest. Blame the champagne for that, but she couldn't seem to stop herself.

He curled long fingers around hers. 'All right, all right. I concede you *might* have a valid point.'

It hit her that they had both relaxed more in the past few minutes than they had all night. And his words should have simply ended the debate. But the clasp of his hand over hers— the way he unconsciously flattened her fingers over his chest and held them there against the steady beat of his heart— changed the moment into something else as his gaze sought hers and held it.

She was going to hyperventilate if he looked at her like that.

His brows drew down and his focus seemed to sharpen on

her. All that notice and attention, in a way that had never happened between them before. 'Molly…'

'We should speak to some more people. We haven't done enough yet. I shouldn't have asked to see that sculpture up close.' She tugged her hand free and prayed he couldn't see how much she had wanted to leave it there, in the grip of his in this room full of his contemporaries.

Molly couldn't be the focus of his attention. If they were both thinking straight, she wouldn't be.

Molly backed away. Literally and figuratively. And tripped over the edge of a chrome artwork frame. She felt herself begin to pitch backward; felt heads turn as she stumbled.

Then Jarrod was there, his fingers around her arm, stabilising her. Smooth words came from his mouth, something about looking at the designs on the far side of the room. He wheeled her about and people went back to their conversations, while Molly fought to get the hot sting of embarrassment off her face.

'I'm sorry. That was so clumsy of me.' Her words were low. 'What if I'd fallen on my bottom right there, in front of everyone?'

'I would never have let that happen.' He spoke the words as though he didn't need to even think about them, and led her towards the edge of the room.

The Prince saved his geeky date from falling on her butt, and led her out of harm's way.

Molly followed. She had utterly forgotten their surroundings as she and Jarrod had hammered out their opinions in front of works of art she would never see again, and could only dream of affording for herself.

Yet those artworks typified the vast differences between them. Jarrod might already own pieces by this artist, for all she knew.

'I think we've done all we can for tonight.' His voice rumbled the words patiently, when he had every right to be angry at his plight.

She searched his gaze and acknowledged the anger was there, banked down beneath his social mask. 'Why won't anyone reveal what they know about these rumours?'

Oh, she knew the answer. Understood it even better now she'd spent an evening among this savvy social set. 'Maybe tomorrow we'll get a breakthrough.'

'Yes. Maybe.' He led her to their host and hostess.

They thanked the couple and made their way outside. The car soon arrived and Molly climbed in. She drew a breath and told herself she could relax now. The night was over and she had acquitted herself at least reasonably well, aside from the almost-falling incident, and the feeling of being an alien, and the over-awareness of her boss.

'All settled? Kick your shoes off if you like. No one's going to see while we drive home.' Jarrod joined her, and she became instantly aware of every movement he made, every sound and change of expression.

'Oh—I don't need to take the shoes off.' What if she forgot, and left them in the car? She did *not* want her boss trying to return a glass-beaded sandal to her. 'I'm fine. My feet are fine. Large, actually, larger than the average female foot. Totally not dainty.'

Zip it, Mollyblather. Right now.

His lips twitched. 'Thank you for that information, though I have seen you in your working shoes in the past three years, remember? Actually, I'd say your foot size is average by today's standards.'

'Well, maybe. Not that it matters.' She became aware of every centimetre of sandal covering each of her not-dainty feet. As though the shoes resented her opinion or something.

She definitely shouldn't have had that second glass of champagne. Molly had just decided this when Jarrod pulled off his suit coat and tossed it into the back seat.

The muscles across his chest and shoulders flexed as he did so, the shirt practically no barrier at all to her gaze. To cap it off he opened his top button and tugged off the tie. Finally he sighed and rolled his shoulders, as though to ease the tension from them.

Molly swallowed hard and looked determinedly out of the window.

To the blurry outline of bushes beyond the car, she announced, 'The brief notes I made in the PDA whenever we were between groups should be useful.'

Business. She really, really needed to dwell on business. 'I'll tidy them up before tomorrow's lunch.'

'I appreciate your dedication.' He glanced at her and, though she tried not to, she turned her head and returned his glance, and the quiet closed around them as his gaze warmed.

'Would you like some music? You can rest and close your eyes on the drive back to your flat.' His voice was deeper than usual.

It tingled over her senses. Molly couldn't seem to catch her breath. 'Some music would be nice.'

Something to fill the silence. That would help, wouldn't it?

He pressed a button on the console and a popular tune filled the car. 'I like this radio station. No talk between songs. That's especially soothing late at night.'

Was he often awake this late? If so, what did he do?

She closed her eyes against the speculation. As they travelled she didn't doze off, just tried to be calm and not think about the sound of his breathing in the darkness, the scent of him…

'We're here.' He drew the car to a smooth halt.

'Th-thank you.' Her eyes popped open, only to find his gaze locked on her face—her nose and eyes and…mouth.

He'd parked on the street between a worn-out green Mini and a family estate-car that was ten years old and probably someone's pride and joy. Their combined value wouldn't pay his car insurance. It was time for her to get out of the pumpkin coach.

Molly reached for her door handle and for words. Something that didn't make her want to turn and take in every nuance of his face and form, so it would be the last thing she saw before she went to sleep. Or, worse, throw herself at his chest and beg to be kissed.

Izzy, Faye and her mum must have put some kind of power of suggestion on her with all their excitement tonight.

'About tomorrow. You don't need to go out of your way to collect me.' Her voice rasped, but at least she was on the right track at last. She cleared her throat noisily. 'Just tell me where it is and what time, and I'll meet you there.' That would be better, wouldn't it?

He named a private auctioneer's rooms, and said they should aim to be there at eleven-thirty for pre-lunch drinks leading up to the luncheon and auction.

Molly started to relax—aside from the prospect of the luncheon part, which could result in fifteen courses and all kinds of social trip-up possibilities.

Her boss went on, his voice deep and low. 'I'll be collecting you, just as I did tonight, because I'll want to discuss strategy again on the way there.' He reached for his door handle. 'Let's get you safely inside.'

He didn't give her a chance to argue, simply stepped out of the car and skirted it: the Prince dropping off Mousyrella at her very ordinary abode. She hadn't even won out about making her way to their next event by herself.

Molly climbed out before he could offer her a helping hand. She was afraid if he touched her right now he'd know every foolish thought locked in her head, every mad longing. 'Um, right. Well, it's not far to my front door. Small flats, small yards, though the back yard is larger. I wouldn't have a dog if he couldn't have a decent-sized yard.'

'I didn't know you had a dog.' He seemed surprised—a little uneasy, possibly intrigued.

And possibly he didn't care less, and was making conversation because her efforts weren't exactly noteworthy.

She hurried up the path and onto her small porch. The overhead light cast Jarrod's shadow against the wall when he joined her. It mingled with hers, as though they were in an embrace.

'Well, we've made the first strike for the business, and the clients we talked to seemed to all relax into your confidence, don't you think? And that man said he'd make an appointment. So, even though it was frustrating, it wasn't wholly bad.' Molly whipped her head away from the sight and her gaze clashed with his.

'No. It wasn't all bad,' her boss replied.

As in *boss*. As in the man who *employed* her to do an efficient and helpful job in his office. Tonight was equally as much about work. Why couldn't she hold onto that?

Because of the way he made her feel, and because tonight had changed their working relationship to something different—and most of all because he watched her with an intensity that meant something had changed in him as well.

'Good night.' Yes. *Pack up the talk and go inside.* 'Thank you. For driving me back and helping me not to fall on my butt.'

She dipped her gaze away from his—but all that did was draw her attention to a strong, straight nose, firm lips, the slight cleft in his chin and the vee of flesh revealed at the base of his neck by his opened shirt collar.

'I guess I'll see you tomorrow, then.' Molly clenched her fingers around her bag.

Please go, before I do something really dumb.

'Yes. Good night and, though you don't have to thank me for anything, you're welcome.' He hesitated and cleared his throat. 'I know you didn't really want to do this, but your efforts are appreciated.'

They stood so close that when he bent his head she could feel his breath on her face. His gaze darkened and fell to her mouth again, and his mouth softened.

He was going to kiss her.

Molly's heart stopped.

But he didn't do it. His jaw firmed, the muscles in his face tightened, and he drew back.

Because she was Molly, and he was her billionaire boss, and this was not a magic night but a working one—whether she had started to forget that or not.

While Molly came to terms with these facts, her boss turned first his shoulders, then his upper body, then all of him to face away from her. 'Yes. Thank you for all your work tonight for the sake of the company.' When he glanced her way one last time, all was in order, the control back in place.

'You— You're welcome.' She wished she could feel half as orderly.

'Go inside, Molly.' He let his glance shift to the door at her back. 'I want to hear you lock yourself in before I leave.'

'I'm safe here.' She turned her face away because she didn't know if she could hide her thoughts this time, if she could match his control or reserve. The burn in her chest was too strong, and danger flashed like neon signs behind her eyelids, because she had wanted what he had considered, and rejected, for that very brief moment. Perhaps not so safe after all from her own thoughts.

'Good night.' She unlocked the door of her apartment, and shut herself in. Turned on the living-room lights, and didn't breathe until she heard him close his car door and drive away.

Then, so carefully each movement might have been planned and double-checked beforehand, she went to her bedroom, drew off the dress, the necklace and the silly hopes-and-dreams shoes, and put them all out of sight.

Dressed in chain-store pyjamas, Molly walked through the compact, functional rooms, and made herself look at the crack in the plaster in the corner of the bathroom, the worn places on the carpet.

And she repeated the mantras that had held her in good stead until now.

Life was not a fairy tale.

Molly Taylor was not Cinderella.

And Jarrod Banning was not for her.

Tomorrow she would hold to all that, and for as many days as followed while they consolidated the strength and position of his company.

He was her boss. She was his PA. And the happy ending would be the resolution of the rumour problems and a strong ongoing working life for both of them.

Molly turned off the lights, threw herself into bed, pulled the pillow over her head and curled into a tight ball. Yes, tomorrow she would get all this completely back under control.

CHAPTER FOUR

'THANKS for waiting.' Molly climbed into the back of the taxi with her overnight bag and gave the driver the address of Jarrod's apartment building.

She and Jarrod had attended the auction, a dinner-show, and this week had put on three group-dinners for some of Jarrod's clients, during which they'd showcased his latest investment strategies and had made it clear he was on the cutting edge.

They were pushing back at the rumours. They'd gained one new client. And they had made contact with their entire client base within the first three days of hearing the rumours and had sent the message out that funds were safe with Jarrod and would remain so.

What they had yet to do was find the source of the rumours, and, through it all, awareness of that almost-kiss seemed to hang in the air between them. And Molly had shopped for clothes. More than she usually did in a year.

Now it was Thursday afternoon. Jarrod had suggested Molly take a couple of hours off, and she'd done so and had met her mother at the mall near her flat for lunch. Since Anna wouldn't be working until later that day, they'd had time.

Molly's brows drew down and tension tightened her face.

Their visit hadn't ended well. Why couldn't Anna listen when she cautioned her to keep her credit card in her purse or, better yet, chop it up so the sales wouldn't tempt her?

Now Jarrod wanted a rush trip to Tasmania. Molly had left a note to ask Faye and Izzy to take care of Horse in her absence.

'Tasmania.' Molly muttered the word as she paid off the taxi—with Jarrod's card—and, bag in hand, got out.

This was a really expensive part of the city. Gorgeous views, big gardens, luxury cars and wide streets. Molly hurried to the front of the imposing-looking apartment building and pressed the relevant intercom button.

Her boss's voice came through a moment later. 'Banning.'

'I'm here.' She hefted the strap of her travel bag more firmly onto her shoulder.

'Come up. It's six-one-two.' Just that. He disconnected before she could say yea or nay.

The electronically controlled glass doors opened, and Molly stepped through into the foyer of the building, then the lift. She tried not to notice the plush elegance all around her.

Her boss's door opened to her press of the bell.

'Why the trip to Tasmania? We don't have any clients there.' Even the air smelled expensive.

'Come in.' He took her arm and tugged her inside. 'I got caught on the phone, so I'm still packing, but I won't be long.'

He abandoned her in the middle of an open-plan living area. A big, swirly rug covered most of the floor area, and looked as though it would be divine to bury your toes in first thing in the morning.

A butter-soft brown leather sofa sat invitingly against one wall. Matching chairs flanked it; there were newspapers strewn about, and a big, tattered book that, from the cover, appeared to hold some kind of mathematical puzzles.

The suite faced an entertainment centre complete with the latest in slim-line television screens. A neat kitchen abutted the room to the right, and there were capsicums—bell peppers—lined up on the bench. Red, yellow and green.

It was so not fair that his home looked not only expensive, totally out of her reach, but also chosen with care, and somehow welcoming despite its grandeur. Maybe she just wanted to feel she could fit in here—Goldirella trying on the wrong-sized surroundings for size.

'Help yourself to a drink if you want one. There's juice, flavoured milk, water.' He spoke the words from a room to the left.

'No thanks, I don't need…' Molly turned that way and registered a host of things all at once. A bedroom with a king-sized bed covered in a dark-navy comforter, with big, squashy pillows and a shirt tossed over the bedpost. Her boss stood beside that bed.

The shirt was his, and as her gaze widened and fixed he lifted another shirt and shrugged into it, but not before she catalogued these facts: boss. Bed. Beautiful light-brown skin with a smattering of hair across his chest. His back and shoulders were firm and muscular.

He caught her glance, and the skin across his cheekbones seemed to tighten before he turned aside to tuck the shirt in.

'What a lovely outlook you have from your apartment. I'll just look—at the outlook.' Molly's breath all backed up in her throat and her fingers tingled. She moved quickly to the windows that faced out from the living room over the city. For a moment she could only stare sightlessly.

When she finally regained her focus, she almost groaned aloud. Because there on the balcony, enclosed for privacy, was a large jet-black jacuzzi tub tucked behind some potted plants.

She couldn't get past the thought of her boss lounging in

that tub in the balmy Queensland heat, glass of wine in hand, bare shoulders exposed to dark night air above the water.

'Like what you see?' He spoke from behind her.

Yes. Way too much.

Convinced her guilty thoughts would be all over her face, Molly swung about.

He gestured. 'The view. It's not bad on a clear day.'

Right. Not bad: as in spectacular, millions of dollars' worth of 'not bad'. 'Yes. It's a lovely view. I like to look out at the view at home, too. There are some great gardens at the other end of the street, and if you stretch your neck you can see a glimpse of ocean way away, in one tiny gap between buildings…'

Oh crumbs, Molly, shut up, would you?

She took a hasty step to the side. 'By the way, you have a great balc— Bed— Television and entertainment system.'

Aah! She needed to pull herself together. What if he read her thoughts?

In fact, he was watching her quite intently and his eyes were narrowed, his face oddly still.

That look—it probably meant he thought she was completely weird! 'I've seen that screen on display at a store and, not only does it create a picture that is so real you feel you could be *in* it, the energy rating on the unit is admirably low.'

Great. Gushing praise and a 'save world energy' speech all rolled into one. Now he definitely would think her weird.

'I try to contribute to energy saving where practical.' Fortunately he left it at that and led the way to the outer door.

Molly bustled behind him, eager to get out of here, and hopefully away from her babbling behaviour. 'I still want to know about this trip.' That was more like it. Something about business, about her reason for being here. Words that had nothing to do with bare skin or balconies or anything else. 'Where are we going exactly, and to meet with whom, and what do we hope to achieve?'

'I'll explain on the way to the airport.' He slipped her travel bag from her shoulder to his, and caught up his own bag from beside the door.

Did his fingers linger for just a moment as he shifted that strap away from her shoulder?

Dream on, Molly Taylor! Better still, don't, because dreams are a dead waste of time. Billionaire, remember? Boss? Other side of the financial planet? He didn't want commitment either. He'd said so briefly, and if she ever did get that far with someone…

Molly cut off her thoughts. They made her feel even crazier inside.

At the last moment he glanced over his shoulder, stopped and retraced his steps to the kitchen. The peppers were shoved into a fridge crammed full of all sorts of odds and ends, and he rejoined her. 'I meant to roast them. I like to pack them in jars of oil with herbs. Great in salads. But they'll have to wait.'

'You cook?' For some reason the thought of him in a kitchen sent her senses haywire all over again. 'I like to bake.' Having blurted this wholly unnecessary piece of information, she fell silent.

At least once they got outside the building she could breathe a little better.

He inclined his head. 'I like working in the kitchen. I sort out some of my best investment ideas that way.'

Minutes later they were settled in yet another taxi, headed for the airport. Molly drew a breath, and so did *not* take notice of the close confines of their shared seating arrangements—

of the way his knees brushed the back of the seat in front of him, or how large and strong his body looked.

'Okay. I'm ready for you to explain the trip.' And she was totally ready to be distracted from her thoughts!

Jarrod watched as his PA turned to face him. That look on her face when he'd joined her at the windows overlooking his balcony! He shouldn't have changed his shirt without closing the bedroom door; he hadn't stopped to think how the impact of her gaze on him might affect him.

Problem: everything about Molly seemed to affect him lately.

Once he let himself look at Molly even here and now, in the back of a very public taxi with a driver right in front of them fiddling with the channels on the cab's radio, Jarrod's thoughts still scattered and he couldn't seem to look away.

'The trip to Tasmania is a business opportunity.' It was, so why didn't he feel very businesslike? He had enjoyed the sight of Molly in his home. Had liked her eyes on him, yes, and that was bad enough. But he'd also liked her gaze on his living space. The whimsical thought had come that the rooms had been waiting for her, that the decorating he'd done and redone finally looked complete with her there.

Insanity. 'Terrence Visi, the reclusive billionaire, has invited us for business talks.'

'That's wonderful.' The brown of her eyes gained a rich sparkle as she responded to his words.

He wanted to capture her expression and hold it. 'Yes. I hope the visit might result in the chance to invest for him. If he's willing to road-test my abilities.'

'If he has any sense he will.' She said it so simply, as though any other opinion would be ridiculous.

Jarrod stared at her and wanted her even more. He couldn't

blame it on the sight of her in a stunning dress, like that first time, though he had found the parade of such dresses difficult these last days.

Yes? And yet you've insisted she buy a new dress for each evening out, though she suggested recycling them.

But Molly had spent a pittance on the dresses compared to other women he knew. She'd meticulously handed him all the purchase receipts so he knew this. He justified the costs weren't even making a dent. 'Your confidence in my business acumen is appreciated.'

'I'm just stating the facts.' She nodded, and her ponytail bounced.

Her glasses were perched on her nose. She had worn them constantly since that first night out. The clothes she wore today were unremarkable, too—a calf-length dark skirt, and a mauve blouse with short puffed sleeves and a wide, square neck. 'You've been a lot of help, Molly. People are starting to look for you at my side, to want to hear your opinions of the investment world, as well as your statistical information. Your take on it is fresh and interesting.'

'*And* full of those boring figures I can pull out of a hat.' She shrugged her shoulders, and he noticed again how fine and slender they were.

'Ah, not boring.' Why couldn't he shift his thoughts from wanting to release that silken hair and stroke his fingers through it? Why couldn't he stop imagining her sitting with him on that soft leather sofa? Why couldn't he simply push his awareness of her out, as he had done on other occasions with other women when it hadn't been appropriate?

'Visi, our host…' He forced his attention to work and told it to stay put. 'He's made his money supplying gas to major cities in countries around the globe.'

'How did he hear of you?'

'Phillip Yates, the man you met that first night and who then came on board with a tester investment, knows Visi.'

Molly's brows drew down. 'Mr Yates was rather chatty when he rang for you. He kept asking my opinion about things.'

'He was chatty with you because he saw us as a team, twice as strong, which was what I intended.' This had worked out *exactly* as Jarrod had intended and, in fact, even better than he could have hoped. 'You're good at my side, Molly.'

'For a complete misfit.' She tugged at her lower lip with her teeth. 'I may be able to spout information, but I don't fit in. I'm always worried I'll do something awful, commit some social *faux pas*. You've already had to rescue me from falling on my face, and guide me to the right utensils and wine glasses more than once.'

'It was your bottom, if I recall, and why shouldn't you fit in as much as anyone if you want to?' He all but growled that last part, and fell abruptly silent in the face of his own vehemence.

'Well, I want these successes for you. For the business. I'm pleased you're getting these opportunities.' She shifted in her seat as though she wished she could get away from the topic.

Jarrod was about to force the issue further when he caught a scent of shampoo from her hair, and something floral on her body, and lost his focus. Instead it moved to a desire to trace the source of that latter scent, discover if it was a lotion or perfume, and exactly where she wore it.

What was wrong with him? So Molly was attractive and he hadn't really noticed that fact until recently? Fine. He'd processed that information. Now he needed to stop processing it so they could get on with their work.

'If we gain Visi as a client, even win a portion of his investment wealth—' Molly began.

'It will very much help to strengthen our business position,' he finished for her.

'Maybe it will be enough and I can go back to just working in the office.' Molly's mobile phone beeped out a message and she drew it from her bag. Read it. Frowned at first, then sighed, and after sending back a quick return message seemed to sag a little in her seat.

Jarrod had an odd tight feeling in his chest that had arrived when she'd announced she wanted to lose the extra hours with him. 'I don't see things consolidating that quickly.' So there was no rush to look at her dropping back to regular working hours.

'No. I suppose not.' She muttered the words. 'That was Mum. I know officially it's office time right now, and I wouldn't usually read messages then.'

He realised he'd been glaring at her, so he lowered his head and spoke, because something seemed to be required. 'How was your lunch with her? I hope my call didn't cut that too short, and of course you can read messages…'

'We had a bit of a tiff over a plastic tree on sale at a shop.' She turned deep brown eyes his way. 'We've sorted it out now.'

Why would she fight with her mother over the purchase of a tree?

'What can you tell me about Terrence Visi? I'd like to be prepared before I meet him.' Molly's words drew Jarrod's thoughts back to business.

'He plays several musical instruments, has his own golf course on his estate, has never married or had children. Made most of his money from the age of thirty onwards, and is fifty-two years old now. It's rumoured he has gold bullion stored in a secured facility beneath his mansion, though I imagine that's nothing but a tall tale.'

'And what about the supply of gas? What countries has he taken that into, that you know of? Were there political difficulties he had to fight along the way?' Molly leaned forward and pushed her glasses up her nose.

The work-related conversation took them into the airport terminal, through check-in and the security checks. They didn't have to wait long in the boarding lounge before their flight was called.

Molly chatted on about company matters as they took their seats on the plane, and then fell abruptly silent when the plane lifted off. She had the window seat, and now stared fixedly out of said window.

'Have you been to Tasmania before? I visited a number of times during the years I worked in the family business.' Not that he remembered that time with any fondness. Better to discuss Molly's holidays. 'Maybe you've been with your mother?'

Molly shook her head. 'No. This will be my first visit. I've done most of my travel on the Internet and in books. It's quick, and doesn't cost anything.' The aircraft made a particularly bumpy, shuddery sound as it hauled itself further into the sky. Her fingers tightened on her chair's arm-rests. 'And it doesn't shake and sound as though its wings will fall off at any second!'

'What you're hearing is normal for this sized aircraft.' He filled his tone with reassurance, because suddenly she looked as though she needed some. 'There's nothing to worry about.'

'Sorry. I appear to have developed a case of first-flight jitters.' Her hands clenched. 'Maybe it's a good thing I've never tried to travel far!'

'You've never been on a plane before…?' He'd made his first overseas trips when he was so small, he didn't remember them.

He would like travelling with Molly. An odd thing to think when they were on a flight that was all to do with business.

Meanwhile his PA was still clutching her seat, as though she feared it might eject her into the sky outside the plane at any moment. He reached to cover the hand nearest him. 'Tell me what else you've done on the Internet. You probably know of some really interesting websites, maybe participate in some online forums?'

'I do. There are some great technology sites, and I joined an embroidery group…' She curled her fingers around his, and drew a deep breath even as her face pinked. 'I hope you don't mind too much, but I can't seem to let go of your hand just yet.'

'Hold on as long as you like.' Jarrod soothed the back of her hand with strokes of his thumb and tried not to think about the softness of her skin. To take his mind from that, and hers from her fears, he started to talk again. 'I've got some Internet forums I visit. Several about finance, of course, but also one that trades in collectible comic-books—and another I joined to ask questions about my entertainment system, and ended up staying because the conversation is always interesting.'

'I've been to the Brisbane Broncos official website.' Her laugh was a little thin around the edges, but a start. 'Mum bought me the kids' pack for my birthday one year. I still have the cap and lanyard, I think.'

'You should see a football match on my widescreen TV. It's like being there, but from the comfort of your lounge.'

'I'm sure it would be. You get season tickets to the games, though, don't you?' Her fingers relaxed in his and she smiled for the first time.

She'd started to forget her fear, and Jarrod was glad. Maybe that was why he tightened his grip on her hand. 'There's no denying there's more excitement at a live game.'

They kept talking. In fact, they talked a lot, just about this and that: things they liked to do, see, think about. They had more common interests than he had realised. And things that made them different, like her love of television chess-matches, and his complete boredom with them, live, on TV, or otherwise. But the differences just seemed all the more intriguing.

Eventually her grip on his hand eased, and then she let go altogether and looked embarrassed, as though realising how long she'd held on.

'Better?' Though it wasn't a good or wise reaction, he realised he hadn't wanted to lose her touch, and didn't want to lose the rapport they'd shared.

Molly tucked her hand against her neck as though to hold the warmth there before she quickly dropped it to her lap.

'Look outside, Molly.' His voice was deep and he cleared his throat before he went on. 'As a first-time flyer, there's something special waiting for you out there now.'

'Oh!' She pressed so close to the portal, her glasses clacked against the hard surface. 'The clouds are like a sea of foam beneath us. That's so beautiful.'

'Yes.' He dragged his gaze away from her soft nape, the curve of her chin and the profile of those soft features behind the big glasses.

Molly turned back to Jarrod with a hundred things to say about the view outside the window. She chatted on and he chatted back; and she felt such warmth inside herself, and that had to be dangerous.

It was. Talking with Jarrod this way *was* dangerous…but also very special. She didn't want the trip to end, and she gathered each piece of new information about him, each small nuance and casually revealed fact, and hoarded them deep.

As they continued to talk, she reasoned they weren't discussing the important stuff, any really personal stuff. So what did it matter?

Yet it did, because Molly felt so much closer to him now. And that feeling stayed with her, combining with her knowledge of his closeness, of the way he'd held her hand and her skin had tingled from his touch even in the face of her flight jitters.

They talked right through the descent into Melbourne airport. He guided her through the terminal with his hand at her back, and only let go when they had to take their seats for the flight to Launceston. She sensed reluctance in him as he released her, and her ability to see danger signals faded in the face of enjoying him, this time together, of getting to know him better.

'Launceston seems lovely, full of character.' She made the observation with hardly a glance out of the chauffeured car's window as they were driven towards their destination. They'd been met by a man in a grey driver's uniform, who now sat silent in front of them.

Molly tried not to breathe in, because suddenly all she could sense was Jarrod's nearness, the scent of his cologne that was so familiar yet seemed so different now…

'Yes. It is a nice city.' He leaned closer to point out some of the city's buildings as they passed them.

Molly sat very still and tried to take notice of their surroundings.

His voice was deep and low as he finally shifted away from her and began to explain various aspects of the Tasmanian economy. 'There's a strong wine-growing industry, and the world's first sea-horse and sea-dragon farm, located at Beauty Point.'

How would it feel if they were simply tourists and could go look at whatever they wanted, take as long as they liked?

'A sea-horse farm sounds amazing. I'd like to see that.' Molly drifted a little.

And then thudded back to earth when she got her first glimpse of their host's palatial home and acreage. The enormous estate perched on a cliff top that overlooked a rough, rock-strewn stretch of coastal shore. Magnificent, luxurious. Intimidating.

'I am so not ready for this.' She muttered the words beneath her breath. 'I've never seen anything so elaborate. The house is the size of a palace. I should have spent the trip cramming on how to behave in a recluse's mansion, instead of talking about football!'

They passed through high gates and Molly looked around. Everywhere was luxury. A tree-lined arbour, gardens that extended so far back Molly couldn't see the end of them. Lush green grounds, and dozens of immaculate outbuildings that probably housed staff and groundsmen.

The car stopped in the centre of a large circular drive. A man opened the car door. 'Mr Visi looks forward to meeting you at dinner,' he intoned. 'Perhaps you'd care to see your suites now?'

He stood back and Molly sat frozen in her seat. She didn't want to get out. What if there were under-butlers and maids, and other who-knew-what staff, and she had no idea how to deal with any of them?

'It's just someone's home.' Jarrod spoke the words quietly, so only she would hear. 'With people inside it going about their business, as we all do. You have nothing to fear from this, Molly, and if anything happens that makes you feel out of your depth I'll be there. I won't let you feel out of place.'

The look in his eyes promised he meant every word, that

she could trust him. There was no place in her defence mechanisms for the Prince to offer to look after her.

She was in trouble, wasn't she? And she hadn't even seen it creeping up on her.

'Right.' She drew a breath. 'I'm ready.'

They went inside.

Molly looked at the ornate chandeliers and high-domed ceilings from the corners of her eyes as they were led up a wide, spiralling staircase. They passed through endless corridors, saw a music room and a computer room and other rooms, until they finally came to a halt before a set of two doors. A painting rested regally on the wall between the two, and Molly knew enough from her study of such works to recognise the artist. 'Is that a real Rembrandt?' She gasped.

'Dinner will be served in half an hour.' Their guide stepped back, gestured to the left. 'If you follow this corridor to the end, and then the left junction to its end, you'll find a flight of stairs. Follow those down, and the dining room is on the right. Your bags will be here in a moment.'

The man walked away, and Jarrod opened the door to Molly's suite and gave her a little push in that direction. 'I'll come and get you when it's time to go down.'

Her eyes were probably as wide as saucers. Jarrod couldn't seem to tear his gaze from them, and for some reason that sent a tingly, warm shiver all the way down to the base of her spine. 'I'll be ready. When you come to get me. For the dinner.'

'Is it— Will you be wearing the burgundy dress?' His gaze drifted over her as though imagining her in it.

'No. I have one I got at a two-for-one sale.' *Right. Blab on.* She sighed.

Oddly, her response seemed to make his shoulders relax.

'I'll see you in half an hour's time.' When he turned away,

she thought he murmured something about burgundy being the colour of madness, but why would he say that?

Molly shook her head and let herself into her suite.

Jarrod knocked on her door precisely twenty-five minutes later to take her to dinner. 'Are you ready?'

'As ready as I'll get.' Molly stepped out and pulled the suite's door closed behind her. Her dress was pale green, a little clingier than the burgundy one, with tiny cap sleeves and a dip in the back, and she felt nervous as his gaze slowly took her in. She'd ditched the glasses again, and now wondered if maybe she should have kept them on.

Or worn the burgundy after all…

But then he fixed his gaze on her face and she saw the look in his eyes, and her pulse flared to life in a rapid fluttering at neck and wrists.

'*Green,*' he said slowly, 'is the colour of madness. I think we should go to dinner. Now.' He tucked her hand into the crook of his elbow and led her very firmly away from that isolated corridor with its two doors so close together.

She wanted to stroke the inside of his arm through the cloth of his suit jacket. Wanted him to explain that comment, though the look in his eyes had hinted at the answer.

'The business.' She wobbled between awareness and unease as they approached a large room, and she caught a glimpse of a mahogany dining-table elaborately set for a meal. 'We're going to do a great job tonight for *the business*.'

'Good evening, and welcome to my home.' Terrence Visi greeted their entrance to the room from his position beside an ornate open fireplace filled with potted plants.

Molly had just a moment to brace herself before the man stepped forward, shook Jarrod's hand and clasped hers.

'Thank you for your invitation.' Jarrod stepped back, rested his hand lightly against her back. Oh, just that one small touch, but she was so aware of it—and somehow her unease receded even while a different kind of tension rose.

Jarrod went on. 'We're pleased to be here. I hope our discussions prove informative for you.'

'I'm sure they will.' Their host gestured them to the table and they all sat.

Molly drew a deep breath and blew it out, and warned herself to stop being so aware of her boss. She managed it, too, for all of the few seconds before he leaned forward to speak to Visi, draping his arm over the back of her chair, and consequently against parts of her bare back in the process.

By the middle of the salad they'd discussed logging practices in the state, commercial fishing and the ongoing viability or otherwise of iron-ore processing, and Jarrod's arm had drifted back and forth behind her more times than she could remember. She'd come to accept its presence there now, with a guilty kind of pleasure that couldn't be good for her equilibrium.

During the main course Molly got minutes into a discourse about literary fiction, tossing opinions back and forth with their host, before she suddenly realised what she was doing and clamped her lips closed. Terrence Visi had a sharp intellect, and was a master at drawing forth opinion and lively discussion.

The older man laughed a little and pushed a flake of salmon steak onto the tines of his fork with his knife. 'I wish you wouldn't stop, but I suppose we do need to discuss business as well as politics and our reading pleasures.'

As they did so and time passed, Molly tried to relax, but she couldn't. Because now and then, as he discussed his work, Jarrod's knuckles brushed the bare skin of her back and they would both freeze into place. But she didn't lean forward.

And he didn't shift his arm.

When she split her fresh-baked bread roll open and reached for the wrong knife to butter it with, Jarrod pushed the right one her way without even a hitch in what he was saying to their host. Molly felt rescued before she could even be embarrassed, and, before she had time to be concerned about *that* reaction, Terrence Visi hit the heart of their business discussions with a volley of questions.

'What gains would you expect to achieve on a short-term investment in your hands, Jarrod?' He sipped wine from the fine crystal goblet, and placed it back on the table. 'Say, three months' duration. What risks do you take and what strategies do you have in place to protect the money you invest? Name your worst financial investment failure, your greatest success and how you learned from each.'

'As far as risk management is concerned, I study. Everything.' Jarrod's eyes blazed with sharp interest as he explained his business practices, his successes. 'My least successful investments occurred early in the business's days, when I tested some strategies and ultimately decided against using them. They didn't result in losses, but I didn't like the risks or the outcomes. I'm probably lower risk than some investors, but my profits don't bounce around as much as a result either.'

Visi dipped his head. 'Considered investing from a sound knowledge base. It's the only way I'll work myself.'

They moved on to coffee before the discussion ended. Molly contributed more than she had expected to, backing up Jarrod's comments with her facts and figures.

Visi pushed the bone-china cup and saucer away from him. 'I will consider this information, and we can conclude our discussions briefly tomorrow before you leave. Breakfast in rooms, I think, and then a meeting in the ground-floor parlour at, say, eight-thirty?'

As Jarrod murmured assent, Visi got to his feet. 'I'll bid you good night.' With that, he excused himself and strode away.

Molly and Jarrod were standing as well. Her boss had helped her to her feet, and his hand still rested against her waist. He let it fall in a slow drop, as though reluctant to end the contact. 'Shall we go, too, Molly?'

The corridors were an endless, silent consciousness until she was convinced he felt this as much as she did.

They stopped outside her door. She thought of him sleeping just a wall away from her, and spoke out words in a low voice that wouldn't carry, even though they were so very alone here. 'Visi seemed open to discussion, but he doesn't give himself away, does he?'

'No.' Jarrod looked down into her face, his gaze lingering on nose, eyes and finally her mouth before he went on, murmuring in a tone that didn't seem to have much to do with business at all. 'We won't know his decision until tomorrow, but we did our best.'

Her skin heated as she stood there, longing for his touch, not wanting to leave him.

'You were great tonight, Molly.' His hand lifted, and his fingers tucked a stray curl of hair behind her ear. His touch lingered against the skin of her temple and it changed from reassurance to so much more. 'Visi was impressed by your knowledge about the business, your enthusiasm and dedication and interest. I was proud of you.'

His gaze dipped, trailed over her shoulders and lower and came back to her face. 'And you looked stunning.'

She should have reminded him she didn't fit in, or played down his praise—but instead she couldn't concentrate on anything but his nearness, and how much she wanted his kiss as his hazel eyes darkened and intent came into his features. Instead she said, 'I'm…glad you liked the dress.'

'I liked it a lot.' His fingers crushed the soft fabric against her skin as he cupped her shoulders. His knee bumped hers as he turned more fully towards her. And then his hands were on skin alone—shoulders, back—in the lightest touch that still managed to hold her.

'Why did I never see you?' He whispered the words, as though, if he spoke them aloud, the spell would be broken. 'Why can't I stop seeing you now?'

Molly wanted to be seen. Oh, she did. And she wanted his kiss, and at last his lips came down to cover hers. One arm closed around her back, the other lifted, and he splayed his fingers beneath her jaw. He tasted of wine and coffee, and Molly melted into his arms because she couldn't seem to do anything else. A touch of fairy-tale magic after all?

He drew her lower lip into his mouth and suckled, and her knees threatened to give way. She kissed him back and his gaze burned into hers before he lowered his lids, and she did, too.

The hard wall of his chest met her breasts, and there was warmth everywhere: in the touch of his skin against hers. Hands, lips. In the uneven beat of his heart against her breast, and the sharp draw of his breath as though this meant something to him, or had taken him by surprise.

With a murmur he deepened the kiss, stroked his tongue over hers, and, when she tentatively stroked back, growled deep and low as his hand brushed across her back and pressed her closer still.

Molly could have stayed in their kiss for ever, held close in his arms. But it ended. He ended it. Shutters came down over his eyes and his expression closed up as though he didn't know what to say to her, and he withdrew his lips from hers and dropped his hands.

He regretted it. She could see it in his gaze, in the way he tensed.

Regretted kissing the runaway PA who had thought for a moment she could pretend to be more. She shouldn't have let her guard down. Shouldn't have let this happen. Didn't want to hear him voice his regrets. 'I don't want— I can't— This isn't—'

'I apologise, Molly. I don't know what got into me.' He opened the door of her suite and stood back, right back, as he waited for her to go in. 'I forgot for a moment. Who we are. The differences. It won't—it won't happen again.'

Forgot she was his employee, and he didn't really want her, and it was only the trappings and the fact they were here, out of their usual surroundings, that had seemed to bridge the gap? Yes, that was what he meant. It had been a problem from the start—the extra work, stepping into his world. It still was a problem, only now it hurt. Molly felt hurt, because she'd let herself buy into the dream a little, hadn't she?

'Of course it mustn't happen again. This was…just a mistake. A result of the moment, of our hopes for a good conclusion to the talks. We forgot, as you said.' She stepped through her door. Turned back.

Added fiercely, 'I don't ever want us to cross that line again.'

Because, even now, she didn't know how she would forget this. Molly shut herself into her suite. Shut out thoughts of her boss. Prepared for bed by rote—make-up off, moisturiser on. Teeth. Pyjamas.

The bed was as luxurious as everything else here. Silk sheets, pillows like clouds. Molly lay very still on her side, facing away from that one wall of separation. She would forget. She would!

What did it matter, anyway? The wall between their lives might as well have been an ocean.

She barely slept a wink.

CHAPTER FIVE

'I LIKE your ideas for my library collection. You've managed to put a finger on what I want even in areas I hadn't realised myself, and how it might be possible to go about achieving it.' Terrence Visi gestured to the books that surrounded him and Molly in the massive two-storey room the next morning. 'My books need just such attention as you've outlined.'

He'd sent someone to push an invitation beneath her door this morning. If she was ready, perhaps she'd like to join him in the library at eight and see his books before leaving to return to Brisbane? There were instructions to press an extension on her room phone to speak with him. Molly hadn't known what to do, whether Jarrod would want her to accept or decline. But the thought of facing her boss, even speaking to him through a closed door to ask about it, when she didn't feel ready to see him or talk to him at all…

Molly had dialled the number and, when Visi had explained he'd see Jarrod got a note as well, informing him they'd meet in the library instead and that Molly would already be there, Molly took the easy route out of facing her boss just yet and agreed.

She couldn't regret seeing the books. She still wasn't ready to face her boss. 'I'm glad you like my suggestions, Mr Visi.

Your library is wonderful. It deserves the best treatment from whoever works on the upgrade for you.'

'Terrence will do.' He smiled, shrewd eyes alight as he glanced at the walls of books. 'I think we've discovered enough of a kindred bookworm spirit between us to do away with the formalities.'

'Terrence, then.' She smiled and hoped all her strain didn't show.

The older man moved his head closer to hers in an avuncular fashion. 'I would like to hear more of your thoughts on this. Perhaps we could arrange some further consultation on the topic?'

'If you think that could be helpful, I could e-mail some ideas.' She hesitated. 'I've read about an innovative new online storage-system that expands on the idea of listings like Shelfari and LibraryThing, with full graphics and room for cover blubs, excerpts, et cetera, but for large individual collections.'

'I want that email.' He drew a business card from his breast pocket, scribbled something on the back with a fancy-looking pen and handed the card to her.

'Am I interrupting?' Jarrod's low voice was the only warning Molly got.

And then he was there, and she muttered something about library listings and tried not to look at him while all her thoughts rushed back to those moments in his arms. But she looked anyway, and he seemed weary, now that she let herself see.

Had he not slept either? Had he thought about their kiss as she had through the long hours of the night?

Oh, get over it, Molly. If he thought about anything, it would be this possible investment deal with Visi.

'We were discussing my library.' Terrence Visi gave a light smile. 'And now I think we should conclude our business so you can catch your flights back to Brisbane.' He gestured to the room's exit doors. 'This leads to a path around the golf course. Your things will be collected for you and the car will meet us at the cliff-top bluff to take you to Launceston. Let's walk, shall we?'

The weather outside was crisp but clear, the carefully tended grass soft beneath their feet. When they reached the view of the sea—a wild, foaming mass below—Terrence drew a deep breath of the salty air and smiled again. 'Magnificent, isn't it?'

'It certainly is.' Molly stepped closer to look.

Jarrod's hand wrapped around her elbow. 'There's no guardrail. Don't go too close to the edge.'

Her skin tingled, and she forced herself to step back so he'd have no reason to keep his hold on her. When he released her, she told herself she hadn't really been affected by his touch anyway.

'I'd like to start with a five-million-dollar investment for the first month, increasing it by five million for the following two months.' Terrence's words took a moment to impinge on her consciousness. 'Let's see how that goes, and at the end of that time we can talk again.'

Then they did impinge and Molly released a long, slow breath. 'That's wonderful news.'

'Yes, it is. Thank you.' Jarrod's face was stern but pleased as he shook Visi's hand. 'Your investment will be worthwhile. I'll make sure of that. You won't regret your decision.'

They'd achieved what they'd come for. On cue, the car rolled to a stop on the road just beyond them. Goodbyes were said, and then she and Jarrod were in the back of the car again.

Only, this time, her boss was remote and silent beside her. Molly wanted to be the same. He'd probably forgotten their kiss already. She couldn't seem to push it from her memory even for a moment. At this stage Cinderella might have packed her slippers up and run away, if she'd been smart.

Unfortunately, in the land of reality, Molly didn't get that choice. Though maybe now she could convince Jarrod to let her ease back on her involvement in his out-of-hours activities.

Yes, sure he'll let you, when he hasn't even found out who started the rumours. Three-faceted attack, remember? You're still working on all of those facets.

Jarrod should have been celebrating, should have been toasting Molly and the success of their dealings with Visi. Instead he sat in his seat beside her on first one plane and then the next as they made their way home, mentally kicking himself for kissing her. Wanting to do it again.

To fight his reactions, the things he wanted that were wrong to want of her, he turned in his seat and made himself look at her. 'This account, plus our other successes to date, will bring our investment levels back to almost where they were before the rumours started. It's a good beginning.'

'I was thinking the same thing.' She forced her gaze to his, seeming equally as uncomfortable.

Maybe they simply needed to clear the air, even though they'd both expressed regret at the time. It was different in the light of day. 'Molly. About last night.'

'There's nothing to say. We made a mistake.' Molly's words were low. She pushed her glasses up her nose. The gesture was defensive. 'We just got carried away by the surroundings, and I was in that dress, and you forgot—we both forgot—for a moment. Believe me, I know my place. I've said from the start I don't fit in, and I don't want to—'

'That wasn't what I meant.' She was better than a lot of the people he knew—more real.

No, it was another kind of difference he had meant, and maybe he needed to tell her that, to seal this off once and for all for both their sakes. 'You asked me once about relationships and I said I don't do the commitment thing.'

'That's fine, and I really don't need to hear—'

'Please.' He held up his hand. 'Let me finish.' He'd never told anyone these thoughts, but now he brought them to the surface, examined them. Spoke. 'Aside from a few friendships I had in school, I can't think of a time when I've exchanged genuine affection with anyone, certainly not deep affection.

'I won't do the commitment thing because I don't believe I have what it takes inside me for it. I'm too like my parents. Blood of their cold blood, a result of their example. That lack is ingrained in me all the way to my soul.'

The words made it sound as though he thought he'd have had the right to something with her if not for this, and he hastened to clear that up, too. 'You work for me. A relationship would be a bad idea for us, even without all that baggage. I…took advantage; shouldn't have. I just want you to know I won't take things there again. I value our relationship and don't want to lose what we have.'

He thought she mumbled something about that being 'an interesting twist in the fairy's tail'. Or something to that effect.

'You don't have to worry.' Her assurance was oddly dignified despite the tight expression on her face. 'I value our relationship too much the way it is to let anything harm it either. Perhaps we both just need to remember this for the rest of the time I have to mix in your social world. Or, better still, you could send me back to regular office hours and hire someone to fill the role of your social hostess and assistant. Someone out of society, more suited to the task.'

'That won't be necessary.' Nor would he accept the idea,

even if it was. 'You fill the role just fine. Things are best as they are.' Jarrod forced the growl out of his tone with effort, and drew a newspaper out of the seat pouch in front of him. Raised his brows. 'Do you mind if I catch up on the news?'

'Not at all. I'd like to read for a while myself.' She plucked the airline magazine from her front-seat pouch. 'I'm sure this will have some interesting articles in it.'

It was a long trip back to Brisbane.

'Right, so we're clear on our objectives.' Jarrod made the comment to Molly as he led her to the sweeping steps of the exclusive members-only club just before noon the next day. He wore navy pants and an open-necked green polo-shirt, comfortable shoes with a good tread and dark sunglasses. He looked gorgeous, and his business focus was absolute.

So be thankful he's taken that attitude, Molly Taylor, and forget everything else. 'We're clear. We target people who like to gossip, people who might open up about the rumours, and we take every opportunity to talk up the business. I have the PDA with me to make notes when possible.'

'Good.' He dipped his head. 'Follow my lead and keep your ears open.' Jarrod took her arm to usher her up the steps. He seemed to have reverted very easily to ignoring any interest they had briefly shared on a personal level.

Well, her boss might be so completely over what had happened when they'd visited Terrence Visi he'd forgotten it already; Molly was taking a little more time to reach that level of disinterest, but she would!

Molly pulled her ponytail hair from either side until the tightening of the elastic band made her scalp hurt. She had on a work skirt, blouse and her glasses. She was primed for business, and this would be fine.

Yes—and what about the dainty black pumps and stockings she'd added to the worker-like ensemble? What was it with her, and borrowing Izzy's shoes lately?

Nothing. It was nothing. Her legs had been chilly though the weather was not…

Jarrod signed them in while she was busy trying to convince herself about the stockings and shoes.

Molly turned to him abruptly, and blurted, 'If we split up, we could speak to more people in the given time.'

She didn't exactly want to toss herself into the shark pool alone, but being right at her boss's side also had its pitfalls. Like wanting to drown in his eyes, and draw the scent of his shaving lotion deep into her lungs before she was able to stop herself.

'No. We stick together.' Had his voice dipped to a slightly lower note as he'd said this?

No, it had not. And, if it had, no doubt he had a frog in his throat. And not a princely one of any kind!

Jarrod led her to a set of three rooms that opened into each other. People milled about in each of the rooms while waiters circulated with trays of drinks. It was a buffet, Molly noted, and not yet fully assembled.

He led her to a group of people who soon proved to be the gossipy sorts they wanted to confer with today. A pity they all clammed up the moment Jarrod created an opening. Two of them looked as though they knew something, too.

The more times they fronted groups of people and got nowhere, the more Molly wanted this issue resolved. For her boss, for the business, and so this could be over with sooner for her.

She glanced at Jarrod as they moved on yet again, and realised he shared her frustration. Her heart softened as she remembered this was far more difficult for him than it could ever be for her. These were his peers, after all. It must gall him to know one or more among them had it in for him, and had managed to do actual damage to his business and still remain in hiding about it—even if Molly fully expected him to rise above that damage. He was well on the way already.

'Maybe the next group of people will prove more open.' Molly tried to sound encouraging.

'Here's hoping you're right. I don't appear to feel very tolerant about this today.' He led the way from the group they'd left, towards another.

As Molly tried to follow, the crowd shifted, and Jarrod disappeared ahead of her. She found herself stuck behind a man's massive set of shoulders, and a drift of conversation reached her.

'I know Banning is indicating all's well with his company but, I'm telling you, my wife heard very distinctly otherwise at the tennis club last week from the man's own mother.' The male voice lowered. 'Know I can trust you with this information, old fellow. We've been through some scrapes together, yeah? It happened right when Millicent went for her OJ after her tennis session. Elspeth Banning was right there, talking on her phone, and Millicent heard her say it—Jarrod was on the brink of bankruptcy.'

'Your wife *must* have it wrong.' The man who responded wasn't a client—at least, Molly didn't recognise the voice. 'Banning's a lot of things, but not the sort to get into financial trouble. I doubted the rumours when I first heard them, and his refutation by means of a display of confidence is enough for me. He wouldn't pull that if he truly had problems. Sorry, but I have to disagree with you on this. Maybe Millicent should get her hearing tested. None of us are getting any younger…'

The first man argued something so quietly Molly couldn't hear it. They moved away then, but Molly's feet were frozen to the floor. She simply stood there, horrified. Jarrod's own mother had started the rumours? Why would she do such a thing to him? *Could* the first man have been wrong somehow about that? But he'd said his wife had heard it, in person.

'Molly?' Jarrod must have missed her presence and excused himself to come to her. 'Is everything all right?' His glance moved beyond her, searched the crowd, though the men were long gone by now. 'Were you speaking to someone? I'm sorry I didn't notice we'd been separated.'

'I need to talk to you. Privately.' Those were the only words she could manage. They didn't explain anything, but after a swift scan of her expression he wrapped his arm around her waist.

'I'll get us out of this crowd.' He steered her towards the door, and out into the deserted corridor beyond it.

At another time Molly would have struggled to hide her response to both his touch and the kindly intention behind it. But now she had to tell him what she'd learned and she didn't know how to voice it.

'What is it, Molly?' Jarrod dipped his head towards hers.

Molly drew a breath and forced out what had to be said. 'I believe I've found out who started the rumours about your business.'

CHAPTER SIX

'IT WAS your mother, Jarrod.' Molly forced out the details in a low tone: the big man with the shock of steel-grey hair and the wife named Millicent. The conversation overheard at the tennis club when this woman had gone to get her orange juice after the session. 'Why would your mother tell someone that on the phone when it was patently untrue and she must have known that?'

'And just happen to do so in front of one of the biggest gossips in Brisbane.' Jarrod's brows drew down. 'If I'm thinking of the right couple, the woman's husband is just as bad. A big-shouldered man, tall, mane of grey hair?'

'Yes. And his size is why I got stuck behind him. He was built like a truck and I got hemmed in.' Molly nodded.

Jarrod frowned, and then said in a voice that was way too calm, 'It was deliberate, then. There was probably no person on the other end of the phone. My mother knew the woman would be there, and that she and her husband would spread the gossip.'

How could he say it so casually—that his mother had betrayed him? In his place, Molly would have been one great mass of agitation—but then, she'd got upset when she and Anna had bickered about fifty-dollars worth of credit-card expenses.

Jarrod went on. 'Elspeth resented my shift away from the family business. Road Ten goes back three generations, as she's always insisted on pointing out.' He hesitated. 'I never considered she would try to force me back into the business, but that's the only thing I can think of: break me in business and I go crawling back. Does she truly fail to know even so much about me, to believe I'd do that?'

'I'm so sorry.' She didn't know what else to say; she wanted to put her arms around him and wrap him up tight and save him from a hurt she could only begin to imagine.

Elspeth Banning's son should mean so much more to her than the family's business!

Two women strolled towards them, and Jarrod pulled Molly to the side of the corridor. A muscle worked in his jaw, and Molly wished she'd never heard anything at all.

The moment the people were out of hearing range, Jarrod straightened. 'My parents are here. I saw them arrive about half an hour ago. This has to be confronted, and the sooner the better. I'll speak to my mother right now.' Purpose rang in his tone.

'I'll come with you.' Molly's anger for him rose in a hot wave. 'I'll make her apologise, take it all back, tell everyone—'

'Sweetheart…take a breath.' In the face of this awful news, her boss actually cracked a very small smile before his face returned to its previous tight and forbidding lines. 'I appreciate your concern, but I think it's best if I deal with Elspeth. I want to catch her with my father, speak to them together, to gauge whether he knew about this. What I need from you is to be waiting when it's done. Can you do that for me? Just…wait?'

'I will. Of course I will, if that's what you want.' If it was what he needed. He'd called her 'sweetheart', and his gaze had softened, and she'd felt closer to him than ever; her heart had melted and filled with sadness and protectiveness and lo— Liking.

'Then perhaps over here, near the door.' He led her to a group of women in their sixties who appeared quite entrenched in a corner.

They had spoken to this group earlier today, and Molly raised her brows in a silent question.

He leaned down to speak into her ear. 'Tell them about our trip to Tasmania. Not the details, just in general terms. They like travel. I'll try not to be long.'

'Take—take care.' Molly stepped into the group and let her boss walk away, but a part of her walked every step with him.

She talked travel. If the women wondered why she had muscled into their group, they didn't ask. Molly couldn't even care whether she was treading all over social toes or not. If they turned her out she would wait right here for Jarrod anyway. It was what he'd asked—but, oh, Molly wanted to be at his side to confront his mother. His father too, if need be. And to offer what comfort she could.

You care for him more now than ever.

Yes, it was true, though she'd tried so hard to make it otherwise. She lasted eleven minutes. Then Molly excused herself and started across the room in the direction Jarrod had taken earlier.

She didn't have a firm plan in mind; she just wanted to get to him. But it wasn't necessary in the end because he was striding through the crowd towards her.

His face was a mask of grim self-control, and her breath tightened as worry for him clawed at her afresh.

They met in the centre of the room.

'We're leaving. I need out of this place before—' He

rubbed his hand down the side of his face just once before it dropped back to his side.

Somehow that seemed far worse than an overt display of anger, than yelling or ranting, or even evidence of hurt.

But then she looked into his eyes and caught a glimpse of a deep-seated disillusionment—not fresh, but ageless, as though it had entrenched itself in him long ago. How could his family be this way? She'd seen his parents as chilly. Now she realised they must be ruthlessly cold.

'Jarrod.' His name came from her lips on a soft exhale. She took a step towards him, probably would have reached for him despite the risk others might see her overture, that she might embarrass herself in the face of an already established rejection on his part. All she saw was the need to comfort.

He stepped forward at the same time, but his gaze had shuttered, and a brisk façade came down over him.

'Not here.' He turned her in an efficient movement, pressed his hand to the small of her back and guided her through the crowd.

Moments later they were outside in the sunshine. Molly took a deep breath, and he dragged air into his lungs at the same time.

She didn't speak until they stood beside his car. Even then she hesitated before the words finally emerged.

'Did your mother admit—?' How could she put it—that she had treated her son with the exact opposite of the unconditional love and support and acceptance a family should share together?

The kind of acceptance Molly had received from her mother, Faye and Izzy for as long as she could remember. A prickle of guilt came to her as she thought of the times she had perhaps not returned that acceptance quite as well as she should have. That she'd maybe blamed them for their faults a little too much...

But this wasn't the same. Her concerns were legitimate, and all she'd ever done was try to make the three women understand they couldn't live in a dream world; it wouldn't pay the bills when they no longer had jobs. Molly *cared* about them. She was no Elspeth Banning!

'No. That would have been too much to expect. But I saw the truth in Elspeth's eyes, and my father has never been as good at guarding his tongue.' He leaned around her to open the passenger-side door ready for her to get in. 'He muttered I should have stayed three years ago, done my duty by the family empire, and by association by them, and then they wouldn't have been forced to take drastic measures to bring me to heel.

'Apparently they'd been waiting for me to grow bored with my "little venture" and get back to what they perceived as my true calling, and, when I didn't, they decided to force the issue.'

'And what about their duty to you as their son?' She glanced around and lowered her voice as she realised she'd all but shouted. 'That day they saw you, they knew…'

Jarrod eased her into the car, crossed in front, got into his seat and started the engine. As it idled, he turned his head to face her. 'You don't need to worry, Molly. I've made it very, very clear to them I won't be going back, and they won't ever attack me in business or in any other way again.'

'So your mother will retract what she said?' Molly wanted that for him. A full apology, admission of guilt—recompense that wouldn't make up for the hurt, but she wanted it for him anyway. 'She'll make a public statement, admit it all?'

He gave a wry laugh. Shook his head. 'You want your pound of flesh, don't you?'

'Only for you.' She bit her lip, afraid she'd revealed too much with the words that had burst out. 'I mean, only over this. The business—you lost client portfolios; Mrs Armiga is still hedging. All that work to reassure your clients and try to gain new ones, and there's still work to do to bring the business to that position of strength you want.'

'That's right, but it will happen.' He watched a couple walk by on the street in front of them before he turned his head back to her again. 'If I force a public apology from my parents, it will freshen the situation, more rumours will circulate. The whole thing will stay alive longer.'

His mouth flattened in a determined line. 'Though a part of me wants them to pay, that's not the smartest business decision. Instead, I've dealt with them in their own currency, so to speak.'

'How—how did you do that?' What currency would work with people like his parents?

His harsh tone didn't lighten as he answered. 'The name and the family business are the things they love. I may not have the power to disrupt their business, and in truth I wouldn't anyway. That's not my game. But I can give them such a fight over any slight against me in the future, the Banning name will never be free of the mud that fight will rake up.'

'Jarrod…' The backs of her eyes stung as his name was wrenched from her. If she'd wanted to comfort him before, it was nothing to now.

Was it any wonder he believed he couldn't be truly close to anyone? How many other times had they failed him as parents? Harmed him instead of helping him?

'I owe you lunch after dragging you away from that buffet before you had a chance to eat. Do you have things you need to do?' He asked the question in a steady tone, though his expression didn't lighten. 'We could go somewhere quiet, just kick back for a while.'

I'll go anywhere with you.

He might only be offering a crumb of his time and company, but if it was her presence he wanted she would go wherever he liked.

Later she might face that knowledge and call herself a fool, but now she needed to be with him. Wanted to. 'I'd planned to walk my dog, but it can wait. I can take him out later in the day.'

'Or, better yet, we can take him somewhere he can enjoy a good run. How about the beach?' His mouth softened a little from its harsh lines. 'We can call into my cottage as well, and I'll show you the yacht.'

'I'd like that. Horse would love the beach.' Molly would love spending the time with Jarrod. There were still things unsaid. She sensed he hadn't stopped thinking of what they'd found out, just wanted to push it aside for a while. 'And I'd like to see the progress you've made on your yacht. The schematics were amazing.'

'We've left a lot of things out about our lives, haven't we?' He turned the car into the traffic and headed straight for her suburb.

Yes, because he hadn't wanted that closeness, and their lives had been so different. They still were. They were going to get her dog for a run on the beach, and Jarrod would show her a yacht he was building from scratch. He had the money to do that, to own a home on the beach and one in the city, and travel where he liked and build yachts in his spare time.

Molly had the money for dog food and care, and only because she'd allowed herself Horse as the single luxury item in her life, so to speak.

Those differences in their statuses hit her afresh with painful clarity when he pulled his sedan into her very ordinary suburban street, right in front of Izzy's tiny bit of yard filled with very ugly, very cheap garden gnomes, windmills and plaster-of-Paris statues.

Molly's flat sat between the two others, as shabby as the whole complex, and so small.

Jarrod looked at her. 'You'll want to change clothes too, I guess?'

Right. Change clothes. Because a skirt, stockings and pumps weren't the thing for the beach. Get the dog. Let Jarrod see just how little she had in the way of monetary trappings: her TV was a tiny box that sat on the end of the kitchen bench with a set of rabbit ears on top to help lift the reception.

'I'll just run in by myself. And, um, I should have mentioned that Horse is named for his size, and he sheds. Maybe you won't want him in your car.'

'Actually, I'd like to see your place.' He got out before she could argue. 'And the back of the car has plenty of room, and it's not made of glass. I'm sure your dog will fit and it will be fine.'

With no other choice available, Molly joined him on the footpath, and moments later they stood outside her front door. She remembered that first night, the way he'd leaned towards her. The outside of her home hadn't seemed quite so ordinary in the dim overhead porch-light.

Or maybe she'd been blinded by stardust from her first night out among the glittery social whirl he knew so well. Or from the Cinderella dress and her glass slippers.

Izzy's slippers. *They belong to Izzy, and you'll be taking them back to her any day now. And they're not slippers, they're sandals!*

Jarrod took the key from her lax fingers, the indecision out of her grasp at the same time, opened the door, and the next moment they were inside.

Molly pushed her lips together and refused to apologise for anything. *Not apologising. Not feeling embarrassed.*

The sharp breath he drew whipped her gaze to his anyway. And then she watched him do a slow three-sixty turn, taking in the furniture refurbished from second-hand stores, the finished embroideries on cushions and wall hangings, and her bookcases crammed with swap-shop finds and all the books her mother and the others had given her over the years.

'I should have known.' He murmured the words. 'Should have known it would be like this, so warm and vibrant.'

While she blinked back an absurd rush of pleasure, his fingers caressed the edge of the cushion tucked into the end of her ratty sofa. He traced the tiny stitchwork before his gaze came back to her, dark and thoughtful. 'You made this? And the others? I'll bet you've read all the books on those shelves, too.'

'Some of them many times over, and, yes, I made the cushion embroideries and the wall hangings and the window blind.' When he just stood there, apparently arrested into place, she blabbed on. 'That's me. Nimble fingers and a sponge for a brain.'

At least she stopped herself before she could explain the difference between the Hardanger-embroidered blind in her kitchen and the counted-thread decorations on the cushions.

'I'll—I'll get changed. In the bedroom.' Her face bloomed as she thought of flinging her clothes off just paces away from him. Of looking at his bare back when he had changed his shirt at his apartment, that was everything this place wasn't. 'I mean just, you know, some Capri pants or something.'

Oh, heck.

Molly flapped a hand towards her sofa. 'Make yourself, um, have a seat. I'll be right back.'

She bolted. Shut herself into her room, where she drew a deep breath and commanded herself to calm down.

At least the flats on either side were quiet. Molly didn't think she could cope with a visit from Izzy or Faye right now.

Molly donned a pair of denim jeans, and a fitted tan T-shirt with a floral design etched around the yoke in gold thread, and slipped on her sensible shoes.

She hurried back out to join her boss. The best thing now would be to get out of here. 'I'll, uh, Horse is in the back yard.' As if he'd be some place else! Perched on top of a lamp-shade maybe?

'Great.' He pushed a book back into one of the shelves. It was one of many second-hand encyclopaedias she had read from cover to cover, and had marked up with sticky notes and comments on things that interested her. He smiled. 'I can see dinner conversation with you would never be dull.'

'I like information. It keeps me stimulated. I mean, intel-lectually.' Right. That was it. She grabbed Horse's lead from the end of the sofa, and wondered if she could hide in the yard until her face stopped flaming.

To his credit, her boss barely blinked when he saw Horse. Her pet *was* kind of ugly when it came down to it, as well as being enormous. His floppy ears and feathery tail seemed too small for the rest of him, and his fur was the colour of a tor-toiseshell-cat's coat.

His eyes were squinty, too. Silly and squinty and always adoring.

'Good boy.' Molly gave him a pat and watched his big body wiggle in pleasure. 'You're a clever dog, aren't you?'

'Do I need to make friends with him before he gets in the car?' Jarrod watched the dog's wiggling antics with a wry smile.

'Horse, this is Jarrod. Be friendly.' Molly laid her hand

on Jarrod's arm as she spoke. She told herself it was so Horse would understand her command, but in truth her dog loved everyone.

As though to prove it, Horse let out a happy bellow of a woof that could have been heard three blocks away and shoved his nose into Jarrod's hand for a pat.

Jarrod gave a low laugh, offered the obligatory pat, and then strode to the door, opened it and waited. 'Let's get him into the car before he pulls your arms out of their sockets with that lead.'

While Molly quickly pulled the flat's door closed, Jarrod went ahead and opened the back door of the car.

On cue, Horse leaped in.

With her dog's head hanging out of the partially opened window, and his deep bays greeting everything they passed, they made the drive towards a very upscale area of beachfront.

Jarrod passed his mobile phone to her. 'There's a fish-and-chip shop, The Crusty Crab. Can you find them in my numbers-listing and order for us? Battered catch of the day, double of chips, and…half a dozen pieces of grilled fish for the dog? And two coffees.'

'No problem.' Molly found the number, and placed the order. His phone carried the scent of his aftershave. She flipped it shut and ran her fingers over the casing, closed her eyes and drew a deep breath. 'You know Horse will go mad at the smell of food in the car.'

'We'll shut the food away from him.'

That was what they did. And then they were out of the car on a gorgeous bluff overlooking fathoms and fathoms of rolling blue sea and soft, grainy sandy beach. They fed Horse, sat at the small wooden picnic-table and ate their meal, then sat there sipping their coffee while the dog sniffed about.

'Let's give him a run.' Jarrod glanced at the dog and patted his own flat tummy. 'I could do with a chance to walk some of that off.'

'You don't need to lose any weight.' Her glance moved over him before she could stop herself. He was perfect.

'Nor do you, but I think we'd better go anyway.' He helped her to her feet and his hand lingered on hers.

Molly Mermaid and the dog-walker Prince made their way to the beach. The Prince threw a piece of driftwood for her pet. The dog gambolled after the wood, leaving crater-sized footprints in the sand.

'Horse has never visited the sea before.' Her pet was barking at the receding waves, tail wagging.

Molly brushed her hands down her thighs and looked away from her boss. 'I never took him as a puppy, and then he got so big, and I don't actually get out this way much myself.'

She stopped before she could give a detailed explanation of Horse's rise from puppyhood to full-grown status, or explain she tried to save on public-transport costs, and wasn't sure if they'd take Horse anyway...

They walked for half an hour, talking sporadically or not at all, while Jarrod threw a stick for the dog until Horse ran off his exuberance and came to them, panting and with a big doggy grin on his face, his stick abandoned.

'He's probably thirsty.' Jarrod gestured to a path leading up to a glimpse of a cottage. 'Let's go up. We'll give him some water, let him take a rest while I show you the yacht.'

He started up the path towards his home, and held his hand out to help her as they began the climb.

Molly clasped that hand and became lost in the feel of warm, dry skin against her palm as he tugged her upward. Ping-pong emotions were doing their thing again, and his touch threatened all her good resolutions and determination to keep her unwelcome feelings for him far away.

He'd needed this time. She had too, and she'd given it willingly, glad to be a part of it—but now the tension rose in the air between them again and she didn't know how to overcome it.

What did he feel? Was he aware of her that way still, or was it her longings getting in the way?

They arrived at the top of the path, and Molly stared at the cottage waiting for them. The front yard held hardy bushes and shrubs, and a scraggle of what could be well-kept lawn, with rather a lot of attention to detail.

The cream and blue paintwork was tired, the sash windows old-fashioned, and the big, wide veranda cluttered with fishing tackle and bits of lumber, a bucket and a handful of tools.

He was a messy boatbuilder, then, and his cottage could do with some TLC to make it into a home. Molly loved it on sight.

Jarrod let them in through the gate, picked up the bucket from the veranda and led the way around the side to the huge back yard. He filled the bucket with water and Horse dived nose-first into it, lapping greedily.

But Molly's gaze was fixed on the car-port style structure of corrugated-iron roof with supports but no enclosed sides. The yacht was there, and it had obviously been a work of effort, time and commitment. 'You've finished. It's amazing. Gorgeous.'

He gestured. 'There's a small amount of touching up still to be done, but, yes, it's almost there. I haven't had time for it in the last couple of weeks.'

'Can I see?'

They went onto the deck together, and then into the cabin.

'What about a drink? I can make it here.' At her nod, he set to work to make coffee for them.

The functional space served as table and bench seating by day, and double bed by night. Molly pushed the bed thought away, though the cabin seemed to shrink in proportions before she quite managed the feat, and she became very aware of her boss's masculine presence in it.

The kitchenette was miniscule, but it worked, and there was a fully equipped bathroom tucked behind a door. More images—shower images.

Touches of his personality were in the attention to detail: the choice of dark polished wood for the cabinets, the scatter of newspapers and financial pages. A set of dumbbells lay casually on the floor, as though he'd used them while thinking over the project.

To work out, to hone the muscles in his arms, chest, tummy and...

'Coffee's ready.' He swung round before she had time to shift her gaze from where it had been examining a part of him somewhat lower than that muscled back.

The silence that filled the cabin was laced with her embarrassment, and his conscious stillness. A heartbeat later his gaze flared, and his face tightened even as his fingers wrapped all the more strongly about the handles of two lidded travel-mugs.

'We should—we should drink those on the deck,' she muttered, and, grabbing one of the cups from him, she made her way there and prayed her face would cool off before he looked at her again.

A bench seat was fixed to the yacht's deck. Molly sat on it and her boss came down beside her.

'Jarrod—about what your mum did to you...' She tightened her fingers around her coffee cup and watched Horse sniffing about Jarrod's big yard. 'I wish it hadn't happened. I'd do anything to change that it did.'

He turned his upper body, caught and held her gaze with his. 'You were very fierce about it back there, when we first found out.'

Fierce and protective of him. Yes. She pressed her lips together but words still plunged out. 'Now more than ever I want to show nothing can break you, that your business is as strong as you are and always will be.'

'We're already doing that.' Though he said it gently, there was a light in his eyes that spoke of his determination.

'I know. And I'm…glad.'

His gaze lowered to her mouth, to the lips she had just worried with her teeth. 'I've been thinking about the increase in workload. If things continue as planned, that could get unmanageable for you. You mentioned hiring a socialite, but I think the solution is to bring in a part-timer to work in the office. Once we have the business stronger, you can go back to your usual hours, but you'll still need that help, because by then—'

'We'll have a larger permanent workload.' She nodded. It would be a good thing, that return to normality, even if right now the thought made her less than joyous. Despite her struggle with his world, a part of her didn't want to stop being with him there.

He was still watching her.

Molly licked suddenly dry lips. 'When—when do you want to take on this part-timer?'

'Now. As soon as you can find someone suitable.' His voice rumbled and his head lowered towards hers.

Molly sighed, the softest hint of sound, but he caught it and his gaze flared.

As though he couldn't prevent it, his hand lifted and his fingers touched the strands of hair that had escaped her ponytail and now lay against her temple.

Her breath caught. She couldn't make herself ease away from his touch. Molly should have cut up the pumpkin and roasted it in the oven so it couldn't possibly even have threatened to turn into a coach.

Instead, here she was—on the deck of a yacht in the middle of a big back yard, hoping to be kissed even though he'd said he wouldn't do this again. But that was then and this was now, and they'd been through something today.

Jarrod's head bent the rest of the way towards hers.

CHAPTER SEVEN

JARROD kissed Molly before he could stop himself. To offer comfort. To push the confusion from her eyes.

Because he needed to.

He didn't understand that last part, but it was there inside him and wouldn't leave. As she lifted up to meet his touch, he experienced the oddest sensations of reassurance and welcome, security and home-coming.

These were thoughts a man would have if he'd wanted all the things Jarrod Banning had never wanted, didn't believe he was capable of. He'd warned Molly of as much, yet here they were.

He couldn't let go, and so he pushed aside the concerns and focused on the feel of her, the response of her lips beneath his as he took the kiss deeper. For her. For her comfort. Wasn't that enough?

If his heart seemed to fill with inexplicable warmth and give the lie to his justifications, in this moment he didn't care.

'Jarrod.' She whispered his name. Her hand fisted in the front of his shirt. The need on her face spoke for her.

He kissed her again then, a probing, hungry kiss that had little to do with finesse or style or experience, and everything to do with kissing her the only way he seemed able—with all of his senses, determination and attention.

It was more than he had given before, yet in that thought was the knowledge that this was far from enough for *her*.

Molly blinked as he drew back. 'I don't understand why you did that. You made it clear you didn't want—'

Yes. He had. Yet his gaze was on her face—on the soft, flushed skin.

She was so receptive. Completely responsive.

And this is totally not happening again, so forget it.

He cleared his throat. 'Perhaps for comfort. Yours and maybe mine, just a little. It has been…a rough day.'

She nodded and swallowed, and her chin came up. 'I wanted to comfort you. In a businesslike sense of the word. As your coworker and…friend.'

He could feel her constraint, her effort to draw back from him emotionally. He had to let her do that. 'I should take you back. Next week there'll be a further round of social engagements. I'd like you to do some fresh information gathering as well, on associated topics that will help with our continued onslaught towards new custom for the business.'

'I can do that.' She nodded.

He got to his feet, led the way off the deck, and Horse came gambolling over to them.

As her pet approached, Molly drew a deep breath and faced her boss. Yes, her *boss*. 'What's the next external event on the calendar?' She could do this, focus on the work.

'There's a live theatre-production in the middle of the week, and a dinner on Thursday night.' He glanced away from her. 'Then there's a treasure hunt at the weekend.'

'How does a treasure hunt help us promote business?' The other two things seemed very ordinary. She imagined them trotting around Brisbane's CBD with mobile phones, following a trail of clues—that didn't.

'The organiser is one of our existing clients. He phoned me at home, asked me to sign up for the event.' He shrugged his shoulders. 'It's for charity. The entry fee is tax deductible, and goes to a very worthy cause. A group of overseas orphanages that really need support.'

'Oh, then you couldn't have said no.'

'I guess not.' Did the back of his neck redden, or was that just a trick of the light?

Disaster struck, of a kind, during the Thursday dinner. It was a smallish group, about twenty people, businessmen and women and their partners in a function room in a very posh restaurant in the city.

'Will you excuse me for a moment?' Molly murmured the words mostly to let Jarrod know she planned to leave the table.

They'd been compulsively correct with each other since the day at the beach, and she tried to stick to that attitude now. It would have been easier if he wasn't so devastating to look at.

And be with.

He got partway to his feet. 'Of course. There's nothing you need?'

'Nothing.' She smiled. Wished the tedious night were over. The host and hostess were polite enough and the other guests had plied her with business questions. Some had even asked about her personal life, and Molly had spoken with pride about her mother and the others, and had begun to believe she'd passed her uncertainty about all this—that maybe she could fit here, do this. Ironic when the need to do so was easing.

The woman directly opposite her at the table had apparently thought otherwise. She'd spent the past hour casting veiled snide comments Molly's way every time Jarrod had become otherwise occupied. Molly didn't think he was aware of it, fortunately, but it was making things uncomfortable.

The ladies' room was quiet. Molly took care of things, and was refreshing her lipstick in the mirror over one of the basins when her fellow guest walked in.

The woman made no pretence of being there for legitimate reasons. 'Well well, if it isn't Miss Secretary.'

'Excuse me.' Molly immediately closed the lipstick and walked out. Not because she was afraid of this woman, but because she refused to dignify her behaviour with a response.

She was in the hallway, almost back to the function room, when the woman spoke behind her. Molly heard the whisper of a door further away at the same time.

'Nice dress.' The woman moved in front of Molly, blocking the way to the function-room door.

So much for avoiding this. Molly sighed.

The woman's gaze raked the knee-length black gown Molly wore, complete with its red sash at the hips. 'Where did you get it—"Chain Stores R Us"?'

It could have hurt Molly. A week or two ago, it probably would have. But now she looked into the hard china-blue eyes and thought about all she and her boss had achieved, and it simply didn't. Not a disaster after all, but a revelation. She fitted in enough in Jarrod's world as far as he was concerned, and if she could give him that it was all that mattered.

Footsteps approached them fast from behind and Molly spoke quickly, gently, while there was still a chance.

'Actually, I think "Off the Rack For Less" is the new hip place for secretaries to shop these days.' She stepped to the left. 'Would you excuse me? It's chilly out here, don't you think?'

Jarrod's hand brushed her shoulder blades at the moment she sensed his presence.

'There you are, Molly.' Though his tone was cordial, the gaze he turned on the other woman would have fried a lesser being. 'I don't know about it being chilly out here,' he drawled, 'but the company seems rather forgettable.'

While the woman's jaw dropped open, he whisked Molly back inside. And spent the rest of the evening casting warm, admiring glances Molly's way.

They left for the treasure hunt on Saturday. It was far from what Molly had imagined. When Jarrod had finally informed her their hunt would take place over the space of a day and a half on an island off the Queensland coast, she had suggested that perhaps they should pull out after all.

They couldn't, and deep down she'd known that. And there would be people around them. It wasn't as if any feelings of isolation or intimacy would be allowed to develop.

Molly revisited this assurance as the boat bumped against the dock and the treasure hunters disembarked.

She'd arranged for Horse to be watched by Izzy and Faye, and had bade her mother goodbye over the phone, and reminded her she would be back in plenty of time for Anna's upcoming celebration of her birthday on Sunday afternoon. Molly had already informed her boss she would need time off for the purpose.

They'd hired an assistant, too. A forty-year-old woman, recommended through an agency, and whose husband had received a work transfer to Brisbane recently. Lori would start on Monday afternoon.

'Well, here we are.' Her boss spoke from beside her as they stepped onto the jetty.

'It's—it's quite a big island, isn't it?' Not enormous, but not the tiny place Molly had envisaged. 'I take it we'll be searching in a couple of groups?'

'Not exactly.' Jarrod busied himself with their backpacks and didn't quite meet her gaze. He'd suggested she bring only sleep-wear for herself and let him take care of the rest. He'd been delayed by business calls this morning at home, and had called to ask her to take a taxi to the dock and meet him there so he could use the time to hastily pack all they'd need.

One of the hunters said something and several others laughed.

Molly looked around them and tried not to notice the hundred and one things that made this place the perfect romantic paradise. The palms and kauri pines, dramatic-coloured sand cliffs, rocky headlands, sandy beaches and blue, sparkling sea. No. Nothing here to set a girl's heart aflutter.

'Like the scenery?' Her boss lifted his backpack onto his shoulders. 'I hope so, because we'll be hiking a substantial amount of it as we collect treasure clues in our team of two.'

'Team of two.' It turned out they were all in teams of two. Couples, mostly, now Molly took notice. How had she missed that on the trip here? There were only about a dozen hunters altogether. When Jarrod drew out the clues list they'd received, and people started to move out, Molly quickly realised they'd all been pointed in different directions for the beginning of the search.

Great. 'Orphanages play a vital role in many countries.'

'Yes, and the sign-up fee, added to that of the others, will provide enough money for a refurbishment, and food, medical care and some schooling for the residents of this one for a year, including some English lessons.' He looked left and right, and pointed. 'This way, I think.'

Molly shouldered her pack. She'd insisted on taking some

of the lighter things from Jarrod's pack as well. At least exercising Horse every day meant she was relatively fit. 'There aren't wild animals here, are there? Or deadly snakes?'

The thought had occurred to her, and, though she'd researched some of the other nearby islands once Jarrod had told her the exact nature of their treasure hunt, this one was out of the way and little known, and might not match the profile she had built in her head.

'Snakes tend to keep to themselves. You'll be quite safe, though it's always smart to look where you step.' He strode off confidently along the beach, and they began the task of searching out their clues.

Jarrod had insisted on wide-brimmed hats, long trousers and long-sleeved shirts. He looked relaxed and comfortable in olive-green combat trousers and shirt, with the pack over his shoulders that carried their lightweight tent and other equipment. Molly crammed her hat a little further onto her head, and followed right behind him in her cargo trousers and crisp, white blouse.

Despite herself she became quickly engaged as they searched out each clue, made wrong choices and had to retrace their steps and overall enjoyed themselves more than she had expected might happen. They were deep in the heart of the island now, and hadn't seen anyone else for at least an hour.

'Wow. I don't think I've ever seen so many varieties of plant life.' Molly pushed aside yet another tree frond. Fun with her boss, who was *only* that now. So why hadn't her feelings died from lack of interest on his part? Why did she still sometimes sense an answering interest in him as she caught the edge of a glance or a look in his eyes?

Jarrod turned to look at her, and smiled until the skin at the corners of his eyes crinkled. 'Not even in your aunt's front yard?'

She laughed. 'Izzy does like to pad out her gnome-and-windmill addiction with some actual live plants now and then.'

'I'd like to meet them. Your family.' He strode off before she could react to that. Maybe because he wondered why he'd said it.

Molly picked up her pace and told herself to stop looking at the width of his shoulders that carried the pack, the stride of long legs, his feet encased in worn, sensible hiking-boots. She failed completely.

'All right?' he asked a bit later.

'Yes.' She straightened the pack on her shoulders. 'Are we headed the right way? The last clue said to watch for the bird that pecks the leaf. I don't see anything yet to match that—and I certainly hope they didn't mean a real bird, because I've seen hundreds already.'

'Ah, but that's half the fun.' He took her arm to pull her up beside him on a small rise, and pointed to a rock formation that matched their clue description. 'What do you think?'

'I think you're too clever.' She smiled despite herself; his fingers tightened on her arm and their gazes locked.

He cleared his throat and stepped away. 'We'd better get going again.'

An hour before dusk he stopped in a clearing beside a small inland lake. 'I recommend we make our camp here for the night. We can eat, wash up and turn in early. With only two clues left to locate tomorrow, I'm hopeful we're in the running to find the treasure first.'

'We haven't seen anyone at all for the past three hours. Maybe we're on completely the wrong track.' Molly glanced around. The area Jarrod had chosen was shaded by trees, flat, with a layer of sandy topsoil that led all the way to the large, clear body of water.

It was idyllic. And so was he. And once again she was in trouble, wasn't she?

'I don't think we will see anyone for the rest of the day.' Jarrod chose that moment to stretch his arms over his head. His expression darkened as he slowly lowered his arms again, and it was there for both of them—the tension they'd tried to ignore and keep at bay all afternoon. 'I noticed after lunch each couple we saw in the distance seemed to be headed either south or east.'

'And here we are, towards the northern end of the island.' For all practical purposes, alone. Molly cleared her throat. Alone and too aware of each other, and she'd done so well during the week.

Only because she had kept so busy she hadn't had time to think.

'Should we build a fire to cook over?'

'The portable gas-burner will be safer and more efficient.' He set down the backpack and started to take items from it. 'We're only heating tinned food, and water for tea.' At this, he glanced up. 'Not as romantic, I guess, but it's practical.'

The moment he uttered the 'R' word a change seemed to come over both of them. He'd probably only meant it in general terms, but his gaze caught hers. She couldn't seem to look away, and a spark of something that felt a lot like longing passed between them. Yes. Longing, and a strong blast of startled desire that flared in his gaze even as it warmed all through her.

Oh heck, and double heck.

'I'll, um, I'll unpack the things for our meal.'

'Let me get the tent set up.'

The tent went up in record time. They watched the food heat and ate it from plates they cleaned with water from the pond afterwards. The tea came straight from a teabag and was wonderfully refreshing. If only Molly could stop being so aware of him as she drank it.

'Thank you for thinking of the Indian Chai.' She drank the same blend at work sometimes, and, though it didn't help matters any, she was touched Jarrod had thought to pack it.

Her boss did 'roughing it' rather nicely, right down to his choice of location for the night, and still there were no signs of others anywhere nearby.

'We really are all alone, aren't we?' She rubbed her hands up and down her arms as she thought of climbing into that miniscule tent with him. The thing wouldn't fit a postage stamp in there without being crowded.

Panicking, are we?

Yes. She was! 'And it's nearing dark.' When they would have to get in that tent. Together. All by themselves. Here in the middle of the R-word setting, just the two of them. Had she mentioned they'd be all alone?

Jarrod put the rest of their things into the backpack. He seemed to take exaggerated care and, when he finally straightened to face her, his eyes held a deep, warm glow that augured badly for any self-control she had left. He glanced at where she'd been rubbing her arms. 'You're not cold? The temperature shouldn't drop below comfortable T-shirt weather through the night, and I brought us a sheet each.'

'Not cold, no.' Nothing glib would come to her. No distracting words to take his attention away. 'I, uh, I'll appreciate the sheet. I sleep better with something over me.'

Yes. Totally too much information there.

His voice dropped about an octave and a half when he replied. 'I can't, either—sleep without a sheet. Guess we're the same that way.'

The same sleeping habits. Yes. Really what she needed to

think about right now. Molly glanced longingly at the water, but did not want to discuss bathing arrangements. It was bad enough talking about bedding arrangements.

Sleeping arrangements! Just sleep. But she was very hot suddenly, and a cool dip seemed a good way to chill out. Literally and figuratively.

'The water is safe.' He supplied the information with his face turned away from her. 'If you want to bathe. Before it gets dark. I'll go in after you're out. I'll sort things out inside the tent in the meantime. You'll be fine. There are harmless birds. Jabirus and brolgas and the occasional curlew. No crocodiles. No dingoes on this island.'

'Right. Well, that's good. I'll get my things.' She dived on her pack with her face on fire, rummaged around until she found her change of panties and the oversized T-shirt she planned to wear to bed, then wondered how changing into those and drying off was going to work. She rolled the panties up inside the T-shirt and placed her glasses carefully inside her pack.

He passed her a miniscule square of chamois cloth. 'Towel.' And a soap-on-a-rope. 'I, eh, there's only the one of these, so I'll use it after you. It's ecologically safe, so it won't hurt the water or anything living in it.'

'Great. Thanks.' She clutched the items. 'I—you won't come out until—?'

'No. I'll be busy.' He stepped into the tent as though both their lives depended on it.

Molly rushed off with the same dedication. She stripped self-consciously behind the thickest group of trees she could find, and hung the ecologically friendly soap around her neck. The chamois cloth for drying was no cover, and she hurried to the water's edge, dropped it there, and quickly waded in until she was up to her shoulders. The water was warm, the bottom sandy, and she couldn't get the thought of Jarrod, just metres away from her in the tent, out of her mind.

Maybe she should have just skipped bathing.

But the water felt great, and so did getting clean. She went as fast as she could and hung the soap back around her neck walking out.

Dusk had almost settled now. He wouldn't look. He wasn't like that. And he deserved a chance to bathe.

A shriek came from the bushes past where she'd left her clothes. It was so loud and so unexpected she let out a yelp, leapt back, lost her footing, and splashed into the water in a full-body dunk.

The shock disoriented her; she floundered and fell back twice, and her lungs had started to really hurt before she finally got her footing.

Her first sense as she broke the water's surface was of splashing coming at her.

Before she had time to be frightened about that, strong hands wrapped around her arms, and she was yanked up against a chest covered in a water-soaked shirt.

'Molly! Are you all right?' His chest heaved with each breath. Hands patted over her shoulders, her neck and back, before he seemed to realise what he was doing and stopped abruptly.

By then it was too late. In that blink of time he'd seen everything and their gazes had clashed:..

Now he slammed his eyelids shut and snapped her to arm's length. Colour washed high onto his cheekbones, and her face flooded as embarrassment licked through her.

He'd hauled her up naked out of the water.

'Ah…Molly.' His voice was a low, hoarse rumble of sound. 'Are you all right?'

'I'm—I'm all right.' Her voice croaked on the words. She

coughed and tried again, though mortification was crowding through her.

She was stark naked. 'Please, let go of my arms and *don't* open your eyes.'

'You're sure you're all right?' He let go carefully, as though prepared to support her again if she'd been injured.

'Yes, I'm sure.' The moment he released her, she edged to his left and around him until his broad back was to her, and then ducked under the water to her neck for good measure. As this also put her closer to shore, and her clothes, it was a move in the right direction, though her entire body was blushing so furiously she was capable of boiling the water around her. 'I am so mortified.'

'And I'm—' He cleared his throat. 'I— Look, I heard a scream, and then your splash. I thought you'd been attacked, or were drowning. But if you're okay can you make it to shore and cover up?'

Total embarrassment; she was going to die of it right here and now.

'Yes. I'm— I'll go right now. Don't turn around.' She glanced over her shoulder once as she splashed her way hastily to the shore.

He was standing in the water with his back turned, hands up in the air at shoulder height, as though to make sure she could see absolutely all of him was *not* turning round.

Molly gained momentum as the water depth lessened. She hit the bank running, scooped up the chamois cloth like an athlete taking the baton and scuttled to the trees. There she dabbed herself dry in record time and scrambled into her clothes after tugging the soap off from round her neck. She was so agitated she put on the clothes she'd worn during the day instead of her sleep-wear.

There was a slimy patch between her breasts, and she was shivering from shock and embarrassment, and something else she absolutely was not going to admit. She used the cloth to wipe away the soap residue, and, with her T-shirt bundle in her other hand, walked back over to the water's edge and laid the soap down on the damp cloth.

Then she faced her boss, who was exactly where she'd left him. She called across the water to his broad back, 'I—I've left the soap. I'm going in the tent to comb my hair out before it goes into knots, and then I'm staying in there.'

'That—that will be fine.' His shoulders tightened. Even from this distance, she saw him tense.

Yes. She was really, really mortified.

Cinderella flops like a fish face-first into the water. The Prince rescues her, and now they're both so embarrassed and aware of each other they don't know what to do.

Well, she was aware. He was probably wishing he'd brought her to an island with no wildlife on it. Or not brought her at all.

Okay. Message delivered. She was going to the tent. Right now. She hot-footed it there, pushed his pack outside so he'd be able to get whatever night clothing he had with him, and made sure it was zipped up so no bugs could get into it.

She remembered there was a sheet for each of them, and gingerly pulled out the first one she found. Then she finally changed under the sheet into her T-shirt and panties inside the tent, folded her clothes on top of her pack, and tugged the sheet up to her neck.

Jarrod came to the outside of the tent about half an hour later. It was very near darkness when he unzipped the bag out there. She heard some rustling sounds she tried not to hear, and then he unzipped the tent, hauled the bag just inside, closed them in and lay down on the inflatable mattress.

It dipped, and rolled her towards the centre and towards him. They both stopped breathing while she edged her way back to her side.

She should explain what had caused all this. 'The scream was an animal, or a bird—'

'I couldn't find the second sheet in the pack—'

They both fell silent. And then he heaved out a long sigh and rolled over until he faced her. She could feel his gaze on her and, eventually, turned her head to look at him.

'I'm sorry I saw you naked, Molly.' He scrubbed his face with his hand. 'What I mean is, you're very beautiful.' He scrubbed again. 'Eh, that is, I didn't set out to look, but you were struggling in the water and I was afraid for you, and I didn't look any more than I had to—'

He thought she was beautiful? She told herself not to think of the way *he* had looked in the water, with the shirt stuck to him—every line of his body on view—nor to think about the wash of colour she'd seen across his cheekbones, the hard-etched awareness in his stiffly held facial muscles. But it all echoed inside her as their gazes locked and held.

'You're beautiful, too.' She tried for a teasing note that came out more husky than amused. 'And, look on the bright side, we're both clean now.'

One side of his mouth kicked up. 'Yeah. I guess we are. So, about that bird. I'm thinking it was a bird?'

'Yes. Maybe a curlew. The cry came from the bushes. It startled me, and I lost my footing and fell back into the water.' She drew a shallow breath even though her fingers were still clenched around the sheet at her neck. 'Pretty city-girl dumb, huh?'

He was bare-chested and wearing boxers. She'd tried not

to notice, but her gaze had drifted over him for the shortest span until she'd snapped it away.

'I haven't done brilliantly myself.' The words rumbled from the centre of his chest. 'In my haste to pack this morning, I left out the second sheet and my spare shirt. The one I had on needs to dry out, along with my trousers.'

Her T-shirt was oversized, almost to her knees. She eased her grip on the sheet. 'You can have this. I don't—I don't need it.'

'Except to sleep comfortably.'

'Well, yes, but you said you feel the same way.' When she went to pull the sheet off, his face tightened and a muscle worked in his jaw.

'I don't think you should take the sheet off, Molly.' The warning in his eyes was clear, stunningly so, and suddenly the inside of the tent felt very, very warm as her embarrassment gave way to knowledge.

Jarrod desired her. He might say he didn't want to, but he did. That truth had been there before she'd done the fish thing in the lake. It was there even more now.

He turned onto his side until he faced away from her.

'We'll be up early in the morning.'

We're not going anywhere with this.

Did she agree? Of course she agreed! 'Yes, up very early, and today's been a long day.'

In the darkness, his head nodded. 'We should get some sleep. So…good night.'

'Good night.' She turned the other way and willed weariness to come. Oblivion would come with it, and right now that seemed a good idea on several fronts.

CHAPTER EIGHT

'SORRY. I thought I had more room to roll over.'

'Let me shuffle that way a bit so my knee isn't—' Jarrod stopped speaking to focus on ensuring no parts of his body touched his PA's in the confines of a tent that appeared to shrink in size with every passing moment during which neither of them managed to get to sleep.

They'd decided to share the sheet. Well, he had complied, when she'd stuttered out an explanation that involved phrases like, 'Fair is fair,' and 'Shouldn't be looking,' and 'It's king-sized, and maybe we'll both finally get to sleep.'

That had been at least an hour ago. It felt like more.

He'd grabbed her out of the water and clutched her against him in a protective reflex that had plastered their bodies together, and he'd seen every beautiful inch of her as she'd surfaced from the water.

Don't think about it.

Jarrod drew a deep breath, closed his eyes again and prayed for sleep. What kind of madness had taken hold of him when he'd signed them up for this event anyway?

Molly sighed and flipped onto her back.

He was so attuned to her every movement, he didn't need

the moonlight that filtered through the tent roof to know when she shifted, or sound to recognise her sighs. He wanted, almost more than breathing, to draw her into his arms and explore at his leisure every satiny, creamy inch of her he'd seen out there in the lake.

Don't. Think. About. It.

'Still can't sleep?' She whispered the question into the darkness.

'Not really.' Even her voice sounded enticing, beautiful, tempting, when logic told him she wasn't trying to be anything of the sort. 'I'm trying to.'

'Yes, me, too. I'll stare at the moving shadows on the top of the tent.' Molly said it almost hopefully. 'Maybe watching them will make me dizzy and I'll pass out.'

Jarrod bit back a soft laugh, and a modicum of tension left him. 'You try that. Good night.'

Molly stared at the tent roof for a long time. She thought she might at least go cross-eyed, but she didn't get dizzy and she didn't pass out. Pity, because she really needed to get her thoughts off her boss and how close he was right now.

How would she look him in the eye in the daylight? Not only because of what he'd seen, and how that had embarrassed both of them, but because of how much she wanted to throw herself at him. Molly's face heated again in the darkness.

Time passed. She started to feel drowsy at last. Jarrod's breathing changed, and she thought he'd finally drifted into sleep. She sighed and her eyelids drifted downward. Through the slits of her lids, the tent shadows still seemed to move. One shadow came into focus and seemed to develop big, hairy legs and a fat, hairy body.

Molly's eyelids opened again, and there, silhouetted against the outside of the roof of the tent, was a spider bigger than a man's hand. 'Oh my God,' she breathed, awed and repulsed at the same time. Wildlife extraordinaire. 'That's got to be poisonous.'

She didn't stop to think her whisper might disturb her boss until it was too late.

Jarrod came upright in a slow, cautious movement, and even then she didn't know the danger until his arms reached for her, folded around her. 'Is it a snake? How did it get in? Don't move. Just tell me where.'

His body was warm and firm where he held her, and he smelled wonderful...

Molly shifted one hand enough to point to the ceiling. 'It's, uh, it's there.' She barely knew what she was saying, but the spider had changed course and was now almost directly above them.

Jarrod looked up, frowned, and returned his gaze to her. 'It's only a spider. It's on the outside of the tent and we're sealed inside.' His hands rubbed up and down her arms in a comforting gesture. 'We're quite safe from it. I didn't realise spiders bothered you.'

'I'm sorry I woke you.' She wanted to explain she hadn't really been scared, had just commented without thinking, but the words wouldn't come. Her hand rested against his bare chest. She didn't remember putting it there.

But suddenly she was very aware of that fact. Molly went to draw away, but his fingers closed over hers.

'Would you like me to get rid of it?' The words vibrated against her hand.

Of it? Oh. The spider. 'I guess so.'

With a soft murmur he straightened to a stoop beneath the spider's position. One flick of his fingers against the tightly drawn tent roof, and the spider disappeared.

'I've dislodged it. No doubt it's scuttling for cover in the opposite direction.' He came back to sit beside her on the mattress. 'All right?'

'Yes. Thanks. We should go back to sleep. Not that I was, but I fully intend to just as soon as I can drift off, and I'm sure if I close my eyes and wait long enough…'

'I was dreaming about you, you know.' His voice was low and deep. 'About searching out treasure-hunt clues with you and laughing.'

Something inside her shivered in response to that low cadence. 'It's what we did today.'

'And I was dreaming about kissing you.'

That was it. Just a one-sentence confession of what they had both thought of and wanted. She didn't know who moved. Maybe they both did.

But his arms closed around her and she pressed up close against him, and he kissed her eyelids, her nose, cheek and chin, until finally his lips came to hers and he kissed her for real.

Molly forgot then about different worlds and protecting herself, about his parents who didn't love, and his belief he couldn't care. About her family who didn't look to the future, and most of all that she and Jarrod had agreed this must never happen again.

'I want…' *Him. His arms around her, holding her. The beat of his heart beneath her fingers.*

'And *I* want.' With a harsh sound he drew her down until they lay prone on the mattress, the sheet tossed aside, his bare chest against her clothed one, their legs entwined as he kissed her again, kissed her with such passion.

And yet Molly wanted more. Maybe he sensed her need, or simply acted on his own. She didn't know, and the question faded with all the others as he half rose over her, looked down into her eyes in the shadowy darkness, touched the hem of her T-shirt and confessed, 'I need to touch you. I burn with wanting to touch your skin. May I?'

Her breath caught on a hiccuping sigh. 'Yes.'

Yes to everything, to anything he wanted, because he was what she wanted. He always had been. The intensity of these thoughts pressed against her desire, worried her, because she didn't want intensity. She wanted 'completely controllable crush', and somehow this seemed to have gone far, far beyond that.

Then his hands began to slowly move, and it didn't matter. None of it mattered.

He eased the T-shirt away little by little. His fingers grazed her sensitive skin. She wore nothing underneath the shirt, and, though he had seen far more this afternoon, this was different, and Molly looked into his eyes and fought shyness all over again.

'You're beautifully made, Molly Taylor. Each part of you. I could drown in your eyes, and your skin is so soft and warm.' His hands tightened high against her sides before he again sought an answer to a question, this time unasked. She lifted up, enough that he could remove the shirt, and then they were chest to chest.

Crisp, curly hair abraded her breasts. His mouth covered hers and she kissed him back, while their hearts beat in unison and the island night outside their small tent whispered and sighed in the voices of the breeze and insects, and the roll of the sea well beyond their small shelter.

He drew her hand to his chest, flattened her palm over his heart and closed his eyes as her fingers curled against his skin.

Jarrod was muscled from the exercise he liked so much and from outdoor activity. She wanted to catalogue each curvature and sinew, and did her best with the tips of her fingers and her gaze in the blurry darkness, until their kisses blended and, oh, she wanted to believe it meant something.

Then his kisses slowed; his hands came up to clasp her shoulders and stillness came over him. 'I can't do this. I have no right. If we continue this I won't stay with you.' He drew away, tugged the sheet over her, found her shirt and pressed it into her hands. 'You deserve better.'

Molly clutched both, but didn't move.

The acceptance in his eyes held her, frightened her.

'You deserve to be with someone who can care for you, Molly, can treat you right—the way you deserve to be treated.' His eyes clouded as he stared at her in the moonlit darkness. 'I'm not capable of that kind of relationship. I'd hurt you, and I don't want to do that.'

Well, it was too late, wasn't it? Because he had. 'You're not like that. Why would you hurt me?'

'I wish that were true.' He turned his head away. 'This trip was a mistake. One I shouldn't have made.'

And, because his rejection was so complete, she tugged the remnants of her pride around herself. 'You're right.' He didn't want to care about *her*. That she had to accept. 'From now on we need to focus on business. All the time, every time. And, the moment it's strong enough, I need to revert to my normal working hours.'

There was a beat of silence. She wondered if she felt resistance in it.

But then he spoke. 'I'll pare down what social-related things we do as much as possible now, and phase it out completely as soon as I'm sure that won't do the business any harm.'

Molly wriggled into the shirt beneath the sheet. His face was averted and he'd returned to his side of the mattress.

They were both very careful not to touch even in the slightest way now. 'Good. That will be best.'

She rolled onto her side, to stay there wide-eyed for hours, until exhaustion finally got the better of her and she drifted into a troubled sleep.

If her boss slept, she wasn't aware of it.

They won the treasure hunt, and received a winner's certificate. The orphanage committee would be able to begin work on its refurbishment, and Jarrod and Molly...

They tried to ignore the awkwardness and went back to work briefly when they arrived back in Brisbane after an early barbecue lunch on the island with the rest of the treasure hunters.

The weather had turned just after they'd got back as well. Bucketing rain kind of suited Jarrod's mood.

Jarrod reflected on all this as he shut down his computer and moved to the window to stare out at the downpour. Even after everything, Molly had still come in to work with him when he'd asked.

He'd pushed her into his social world knowing she didn't want to be there, made a royal mess of things last night in that damned tent with her. His self-control was shot around her, and he had to get it back and keep it back.

Her reflection appeared behind his, and he spoke without turning. 'At least we didn't have to try to make the trip back from the island in this weather, but I'm sorry I've had to yet again ask you to go above and beyond for the sake of the company.'

'I didn't mind. I want the business to flourish.' Molly stood in the doorway, her backpack in her hand. 'I've always wanted that.' She passed the pack from one hand to the other. 'I'm due at Mum's in less than an hour for her birthday celebration, and I need to collect the cake from my flat.'

'You can't catch public transport in this weather.' She would need to do so, to get home and then to her mother's place. 'Especially not with a birthday cake in your hands.' One Molly had told him she had made for her mum.

'Then I'll take a taxi.' Her chin was up, her gaze guarded.

'Let me drive you to your place and on to your mother's.' He needed to be sure she arrived safely, and he needed to do something for her, to give to her in some small way.

Since holding her in his arms, and wanting so much to make love to her, he couldn't shake her out of his thoughts. There was an ache in his chest all the time. He figured it was some kind of guilt.

Because despite everything he still wanted to possess her. Instead all he could do was choose not to hurt her.

But he could drive her to her mother's in the rain. 'You're running late because I dragged you into the office when you needed to go straight to your flat. Let me at least make amends for that.'

He didn't wait for her agreement. Instead, he swept her out of the office and into the underground parking-lot and his car before she could say anything at all.

'It's—it was convenient you'd left your car at the dock so you could drive us straight here when you got that phone call.' She was nervous of him.

He couldn't blame her. 'Yes. That helped.'

Her mobile phoned beeped an incoming message as she settled in her seat.

Jarrod set the sedan in motion, took them out of the underground parking-area and up onto the street, and headed for Molly's flat, with the windscreen wipers doing double time to try to cope with the deluge.

· Molly read her message and sent one, and when they

arrived at her place observed, 'I'll need to shower and change clothes, but I'll be quick.'

Jarrod had showered after they'd arrived at the office, had tentatively offered her the chance, but she'd busied herself at her desk without meeting his gaze and had declined. It had been a stupid offer.

Her reaction had reminded him again of their exchanges at the island. As though he needed any help remembering.

'I'll read while I wait.' He opened one of her encyclopae-dias from the shelf, and focused on it fiercely until she emerged from her room. She looked fresh and lovely in a pale-blue skirt and fitted black top. Her hair was in the regulation ponytail.

'I made gingerbread cake. Mum loves it, and it needs a couple of days with the frosting on in the fridge, so it should be at its best now.' Molly gabbled the words as she gathered up the cake. 'There's a present as well.'

He took the long, cylindrical parcel and held the umbrella over her again as they returned to the car.

'You really didn't have to do this, but I appreciate it.' Molly settled into her seat, and the scent of baked cake wafted between them. 'What's— do you have a favourite birthday cake?'

She was talking for the sake of avoiding the tension between them.

He did his best to help her out. 'I suppose if I wanted birthday cake I might like black-forest torte. I'm partial to maraschino cherries.'

'I could make that. Actually, it's one of Izzy's favourites, but she always insists on buying one from the most upmarket cake place in the CBD.' Was there a bit of a snap in her tone?

How would he feel if Molly baked him a birthday cake?

Like happy families or something? *Not* a question he needed to be asking himself.

She fell silent, and then her phone beeped again. There were several more text messages on the way to her mother's. Molly didn't refer to them, though her return text messages were punched into her phone with greater and greater speed, until she shut the phone off completely and shoved it to the bottom of her bag.

'Turn left at the next intersection, and the block of flats is on the right, halfway down. The street is long. I'll tell you when you're getting close.' Molly seemed to become all the more agitated the closer they got.

'Is something wrong?' He asked it in a mild tone, told himself he wasn't really curious, or concerned.

Her head whipped around. 'No. Mum and the others are just… It's nothing. I can handle them—*things*. Thank you for being kind enough to help me get the cake to the party.'

No one had called him kind before.

'It's there. The one with the brick mailboxes to the right.'

When they stopped in a parking space, Molly glanced up at a second-floor balcony in the block of flats.

'I told them to wait inside.' She muttered the words under her breath and reached for her door handle.

Jarrod let his gaze follow where hers had gone, and there beneath a garish awning, with glasses in hand, stood three women.

The women all peered down at the car, then burst into excited chatter. They waved, tucked phones into pockets, raised glasses of whatever drinks they held and disappeared in a rush into the apartment behind them.

'Well, thank you for driving me here. I really appreciate it, and I'll see you tomorrow at work.' Molly flung her door open as though her life depended on making a fast escape.

But it was still bucketing down, they were parked on the

street with no shelter, and the cake in her hands was still as vulnerable to a dunking as when they had left her flat. It was a big cake, tall, and shaped like a house. He doubted she'd have found a container to cover it.

'I'll help you get that inside before I leave. Mustn't forget your gift either.' He thought it a sensible idea, though she grimaced and cast a desperate glance towards the lobby of the building as she reluctantly accepted his offer.

Jarrod retrieved her gift from the back seat and went round to help her out of the car.

'Molly, darling, you're here at last.' A woman appeared at Jarrod's side. She was petite, with short-cropped brown hair, brown eyes like Molly's and a cheerful smile. She had a margarita in one hand and a floral umbrella in the other.

'Hi, Mum. Happy birthday.' Molly leaned forward and kissed her on the cheek.

Two more women joined them, blandishing similar accoutrements.

The willowy redhead hiked her umbrella a little higher. 'And you've brought your boss to join us.'

'There's nothing like another guest at a party for the birthday girl.' This was declared by the third woman, who was blonde and looked nothing like the others. 'Come inside, come inside.'

Umbrellas clashed overhead as they all entered the lobby in a tight pack. Despite the half-desperate, half-exasperated expression on his PA's face, Jarrod couldn't help grinning a little.

Molly muttered something about margarita madness starting early this birthday, and that they'd better not talk about slippers. He didn't quite catch it. And then he was swept willy-nilly up flights of stairs, the three women chattering at once, until they stopped outside an apartment and Jarrod finally got a word in.

'I'll leave you to your celebration. I just came to help Molly take care of the cake.' Somehow there seemed to have been a misunderstanding, but he had no intention of foisting himself on what was, after all, a private birthday celebration for his PA's mother.

'Oh. You're leaving?' Molly's mother looked from the cake to her daughter's face, to the faces of the others and finally to Jarrod. She seemed disappointed. 'We hoped you'd stay, give us a chance to get to know Molly's employer a little.'

It didn't exactly come under 'business'. Jarrod tried for an urbane smile. 'I wouldn't want to put anyone out.'

'Good. Then, since you won't be, that's settled.' The redhead took his arm and steered him inside. Before he could blink he had a beer in his hand, Molly had a margarita in hers, and they'd both been urged to sit side by side on a tired-looking sofa draped in a chintz cloth.

The women pulled up armchairs and turned as one to Molly, eyebrows raised expectantly.

Molly sighed beneath her breath and cast him a look of defeat. 'Mum, Izzy, Faye, please meet my employer, Jarrod Banning.' She gestured towards the three women one after another. 'Jarrod, this is my mother, Anna Taylor.' She nodded towards the redhead. 'Her sister, Isobel Taylor.' And finally the blonde. 'Our long-time friend, Faye Manchette.'

'My pleasure.' Jarrod shook slim hands. Anna's was worker-like, the nails cut short, surprisingly strong. They all cast swift examinations over him as they murmured their greetings.

This was Molly's family. He didn't know how they all fitted into the picture, except Molly's affection for them was clear even in her current state of unease. From the last names, it seemed clear her mother had never married.

'We grew up together. We're still very close.' Izzy supplied the information as though she guessed he might have wondered. 'Molly is like a daughter to all of us.'

Right, and Jarrod had been put on inspection, and Molly wasn't comfortable about that. He turned to his PA, and murmured, 'I'll go. They just swept me up before I realised quite what was happening.' He half rose from his seat.

For one brief moment, Molly dithered. It was unlike her, and he hesitated, but then she wrapped her fingers around his wrist and pulled him back down. Her expression was tight and determined and not particularly party-like. 'It would please Mum and the others if you stayed, and maybe I want you to see where I've come from.'

He stayed. Partly because it seemed to be expected, and partly because Molly seemed to think doing so would be educational—though he hadn't quite managed to join the dots on that logic just yet. Did she think he would run screaming because her family didn't have money? The possession of such hadn't exactly done much for *his* family! And he and Molly had decided there was nothing between them, anyway. *Right?*

Izzy got to her feet in a burst of cheerful energy. 'Let's watch Anna open her gifts and have another round of drinks.' She glanced at the gift Molly had tucked against the side of the couch when they came in.

'There's no need to hit the tequila too much.' Molly clutched her fingers around her own virtually untouched drink. 'We can just eat cake and play music and talk.'

But the three older women didn't take much notice of her. A small portable stereo-system was set up to play a CD of what appeared to be a favourite crooner. More drinks were poured and gifts were opened.

Anna exclaimed with delight over some chocolates, perfume and a set of pearl earrings.

Molly kissed Anna's now somewhat flushed cheek and handed her gift over. 'I hope you like it.'

'A Hardanger blind!' Anna made the exclamation as she removed the layers of wrapping paper. 'Oh Molly, it will look fabulous over the kitchen window. You must have put in so much work to make this.' Her fingers traced the almost mathematical design that formed the blind's border.

Molly had one similar to this in her kitchen at the apartment. The thought of her sitting there, painstakingly creating such things, made something twist in Jarrod's chest.

She was his geek-girl secretary. She loved information and technology and clearly her family, whether they exasperated her for unknown reasons or not. Apparently she also liked… nesting.

One day she would want a family of her own. The thought jarred him. He didn't want to imagine her with someone…

Jarrod's mouth tightened, and Molly turned to him.

'Is everything all right?'

'I'm the only person not bearing a gift. It seems wrong.'

'The gift is your presence to join in our fun.' Faye toasted him with her drink. 'We were there the first night you and Molly went out, you know. Helped her choose her shoes.'

'Went out on business.' Molly cut in to clarify. 'And there's no need to talk about that. It's time for Mum to cut the cake.'

For the next hour they laughed and chatted, asked questions about Jarrod's business and talked about their jobs. They did low-pay work, but they seemed content, and they were incredibly proud of Molly. That came out in a hundred different ways.

A different kind of family, with three ladies who'd banded together to raise one girl into the woman who sat beside him on the couch now. Molly had downed her drink and now nursed a second. That had happened when her mother had started talking about potty training her when she was a toddler. Jarrod hid a smile.

They played Scrabble. Listened to more music. Drank more margaritas—the other three, not Molly—and Jarrod stuck to his one beer.

Things got chattier, sillier. When the game of Scrabble ended, and Faye and Izzy started singing along to the music while her mother muttered about bringing out the photo albums, Molly got to her feet.

'This has been wonderful, but I'm sure Jarrod needs to get back to his place, and I need to go home to Horse and make it up to him for leaving him in a soggy back yard for so long without even a hello.'

Jarrod came to his feet beside his PA. 'Can we offer anyone a lift?'

'That would be a change to taking a bus.' Faye nodded.

Izzy did the same.

Hugs and kisses were exchanged. Jarrod received his share. He blamed the tequila, but even so it felt rather odd and ridiculously warming to be treated with such easy affection, as though he'd been accepted simply because he was with Molly.

As her boss. You have to remember that.

Moments later Anna had waved them off in the now steamy late-afternoon's watery sun, and Jarrod, Molly, Izzy and Faye were headed back to their flats in his car.

Molly's elders gave quite unnecessary directions on the way and, when they approached their destination, fell to whispering in the back seat.

He heard snippets such as: 'Leave them alone to say goodbye. You never know.'

And, 'I think he likes her. Did you see how he watched her?'

The moment he drew the car to a stop they climbed out.

'Thanks for the lift.'

'We won't keep you.'

'Drop by for breakfast in the morning, Molly.'

The women disappeared into one of the apartments, arms linked, and closed the door behind them with a bang.

Molly let out a deep gust of breath and leaned her head back against the headrest for a moment before she sat up straight. 'It's a family ritual. They like to drink margaritas and pretend... Well, whatever they choose on the day.' She shrugged her shoulders. 'Rather different from what you're used to, I'd imagine.'

'They're proud of you and they...love you.' That was what had come through to him. Not tequila or bad music, but the way the women had talked Molly up to him every chance they'd got.

If Molly had wanted him to see the differences, fine, he'd seen them. Her family were salt-of-the-earth people. His parents wanted to own real-estate. But it was the differences of caring and closeness that truly divided he and Molly. That fact was cuttingly plain to him right now—more than he had ever seen of himself, of where *he* had come from—and he suddenly felt quite grim.

'Your family seem like wonderful people.' He made certain the words were no more than an observation, a careful one, and he went on because he at least wanted to understand this. 'Yet you seem to get uptight about them sometimes. You mentioned an incident to do with a plastic tree. The one in your mother's living room?'

Her gaze flew to his, full of confusion and unease, before she waved a hand. 'That was nothing, really, and today they were just dreaming up all these elaborate ideas for Mum's birthday and sending them to me by text message. Like going out for high tea at Brisbane's answer to the Ritz. It would have cost a bomb. They, well, they settled down when I reminded them I'd baked a cake and was looking forward to having that with them.'

It was an answer and not an answer, but she didn't owe him anything more, even if he wished she had chosen to confide in him more fully. Perhaps he could have helped.

Yeah—long shot, Banning. Really long, given you wouldn't have a clue.

He still didn't like that she was shutting him out, though she had every right to hold on to her privacy.

'I enjoyed getting to know them.' He stuck to that, and it was quite true. He couldn't imagine his mother cackling with laughter over a board game, or telling tales about his childhood.

'I have to go.' His words were clipped, low, as he pulled his thoughts back.

'Yes. I thought you might feel that way.' On this announcement, that tightened her mouth and her face, she climbed from the car. 'I'll see you tomorrow. At work.'

She hurried away up the small pathway to her flat, went inside and closed the door without looking back.

CHAPTER NINE

MOLLY rose earlier than usual Monday morning, put Horse on his lead, and gave him a run for his money. When they got back to her flat they were both breathing hard, and Molly had herself sorted out.

She had got off track with her boss, rather majorly a couple of times, but that didn't have to be an issue any more. Bottom line? He wasn't interested in her personally, and she would be best only to care about their work. She would start by training in their new employee this afternoon.

Molly would be a great PA. She would do that, one hundred and fifty percent, and Jarrod would make sure there weren't many more social events.

She sat on the bus now, headed for the office. No more dreams, either. No more Cinder-sandals thoughts.

She got off the bus and made her way to their building. Jarrod wasn't behind his desk when she let herself in. The rear door of his office was open. She could hear sounds back there. Maybe he was dressing after a shower. Molly didn't want to know. She turned on her computer, stowed her bag in the drawer, took the phone off answering service and didn't think about noises.

He'd seen her naked; they'd almost made love.

No. She wouldn't think of it.

'I hope your family roused themselves okay this morning, after their partying.' His words were a stab at determined cheerfulness that didn't reach his guarded eyes.

It didn't matter. They were doing this. Molly gave a polite smile, and didn't quite meet his gaze. 'My mother and the others are fine.'

'Glad to hear it.' He cleared his throat. 'I have some business-related news that's a little on the ironic side.'

'Good or bad news?' She could do with something good.

'Some assessing work that will pay well and might lead to a new portfolio for us. The possibility's been mentioned.' His brows drew down a little. 'The irony part is that the man contacted me because he's been dealing with my parents.'

'That is ironic.' Her voice sounded wistful even over this. She hated that fact. Swallowed, and sat up straighter.

Brows drawn together, he moved to stand beside her chair. 'Molly—'

'I'm glad you have a lead.' No pity. No understanding glances. She absolutely would not accept those things. She pushed the chair back and climbed to her feet, maybe because she needed to look at him from a stronger position than sitting.

Not because it brought them closer together, though she noticed he didn't step back at all.

Not relevant! 'Will it mean a dinner? I can buy another dress, or wear one I've worn before. I don't care. It's all the same to me. Or is it something you don't need me along for? That would be even better.'

Completely better. Totally better. Exactly what would be best for all concerned.

The outer-office door pushed open. Stuart and Elspeth stood there.

'What are you doing here?' Jarrod moved away from her in increments. One step, two. He didn't round the desk. Made no attempt to get closer to the older couple as they stepped right into the room.

Molly's feet covered the distance that separated her and her boss. She moved in close to his side.

'Road Ten's deal with the king…' Stuart Banning didn't seem to care about his son's lack of welcome, about Molly's movement to stand close to her boss.

He gave no introductory greeting. No 'I'm so sorry we tried to damage you in business' speech. It was as though that was no longer relevant in his mind as he focused on some comment about a king.

It was still very relevant to Molly's boss, and by association to her. Molly's blood pressure did a slow climb.

But Stuart Banning simply went on. 'The king invited us back for a second round of talks. We'd anticipated this, but not his announcement that you would be there visiting as well.' Accusing tone, narrowed eyes. 'What did you do? What have you told him? We agreed to stay out of your way, to leave you be. If our negotiations break down now—'

'It must be my day for ironies.' Jarrod gave a small shake of his head, as though at the wiles of fate, before his tone hardened. 'I know nothing of you and Elspeth visiting the king a second time. If he's invited you, I suggest you put off the visit to another time. I'm afraid I've already booked my flights.'

Elspeth Banning stood at her husband's side. Her face was tight. 'How could the king know about you if it wasn't that you contacted him?'

'He learned about me when he investigated both of you. Surely you expected a bit of a probe? If you want the man to do business with you…' Jarrod shrugged his shoulders. 'His call to my apartment last night surprised me. He didn't mention the two of you would be visiting at the same time. Maybe he's under the mistaken impression we're close. As we're not, and I'm not interested in your business dealings, you have no reason to fear my presence there.'

'Well, this would have been far easier to discuss if you'd answered your father's calls to your mobile phone this morning,' Elspeth snapped. 'All he got was your message bank. You should always answer, be immediately contactable, in case of emergency.'

Do you think Faye would have a pair of sandals I could wear with a burgundy evening-dress?

Molly had texted her mother in the full assurance Anna would have her phone on her hip or close by, no matter what had occupied her, just because Molly, Izzy or Faye might want to contact her.

Now Jarrod's mother was demanding he make himself constantly available to her, citing her business woes as 'emergency' material. Anger balled in Molly's chest and begged to be let out.

'I listen to every message left on any of my phone services.' Jarrod spoke the words in a low tone. 'If any call came through that meant either of you were in danger, in hospital or something, I would come.'

'That's not the point!' Elspeth rejected this overture without apparently even seeing it for what it was. 'These are *our* business efforts. You can't simply muscle in—'

'Like you did against mine?' He drew a breath. Shook his head. Turned to his father. 'What do you want me to do about this? I have dealings of my own with the king. I'm not about to cancel the arrangements.'

Elspeth puffed up like a blower fish. 'That's exactly what you must do. We don't want to share the attention.'

Molly wanted to say all kinds of things—threaten *their* livelihoods, maybe suggest a hair-ripping contest. Elspeth's...

'Not happening.' Jarrod pushed his hands deep into his trouser pockets. They were curled into fists. 'And I guess, if neither of you is prepared to back out for a few days, that's all there is to be said. I'm sure we can all manage to be civil over there.'

Protectiveness swelled in Molly's chest. She turned to him and said in a low voice, so the others wouldn't hear, 'You don't have to spend time with them. You can call the king, say you'll go later.'

'It will be okay, Molly.' He drew his hand from his pocket and surprised her by curling his fingers around her wrist. 'Besides, if I don't go, I'll feel like they're winning, and I really don't want to have that feeling.'

And her heart hurt all the more. For him, for his belief he couldn't have more than the horrid relationship his parents had with him, and no doubt with each other. She hadn't truly faced that history of his, not fully, until now. 'When—when do you leave?'

'I need to leave soon, actually.' He released her wrist, stepped away and turned to his parents. 'I have no interest in your business dealings whatsoever. You might try to remember that before you come barging in here again. Go to see the king now, or don't. I really don't care one way or the other. Now, I need to leave Molly with some instructions before I catch my flight.'

He held the outer-office door open and waited.

'Then we go now.' Stuart Banning strode towards the door first. 'Our jet is waiting.'

After a brief hesitation, Elspeth wisely closed her thin lips and followed.

Jarrod gave Molly his instructions.

'I expect to be gone several days.' He collected a travel bag, and hesitated with his hand on the wall beside the outer door. His gaze roved her face, seemed to take in each part of her before he turned away. 'Take care of yourself, Molly.'

'You—you please do the same.' She drew a breath. 'I'll look after the business for you while you're gone.'

But who would look out for him?

CHAPTER TEN

JARROD stared out of the plane's window. It was Friday. He had spent the working week overseas with the king's financial advisory team. He'd probed, made suggestions, found some weak areas in certain investments, and had been generously rewarded for his input. The king hadn't offered him any investment monies to handle for him, but he was thinking about it. Overall, a good result.

Molly would be pleased about the payment Jarrod had netted for his services. She hadn't left his thoughts this week. Soon he would be back with her.

Yes. In a business sense only.

His parents' negotiations with the king appeared to have gone well. Jarrod had done his best to stay out of their company, and for the most part that had worked.

When the plane came in to land he decided it was just as well it was the weekend, with no chance of seeing his PA at the office. He would be better to go to his cottage and work on his yacht, and blow off this weariness with some outdoor work. He would see Molly on Monday. That would be soon enough.

He did work on the yacht, but it was already seaworthy, and all it needed was a bit of polish here and there. That took less than two hours of his Friday evening.

The king phoned Jarrod for further talks three times during the course of the Saturday. Jarrod hunkered in and lost himself in those talks because, it was better than thinking about things he couldn't think about—of PA's with big brown eyes and pets the size of houses.

On Sunday morning he had the yacht transported to the nearby marina where it would rest when he wasn't using it.

He followed in his car, saw things organised with the yacht, and then his mobile phone rang.

Five minutes later, he had sealed a deal that would put his business back into very firm standing indeed.

Molly would be pleased. And he wanted to see her. For the business. To celebrate this. Jarrod made several phone calls, and then made one more.

'Molly. Hi.' His tongue threatened to tie itself into a knot, as though he were a schoolboy in the throes of a crush. 'Eh, it's me.'

'Hi. I've miss— How are you?' Her voice was guarded and careful, and the best thing he'd heard in days.

'Well. I'm well.' *Now that I'm hearing your voice.* 'I just got an investment offer from the king that's enough to make your eyes glaze over.' He told her the amount, and explained the details briefly.

And then drew a deep breath and closed his eyes. 'So, I thought we should celebrate. The yacht is finished, and I have it at the marina near my place. There's—there's a taxi on the way to get you and Horse, if you're free to come. Dress would be casual, with sunscreen, swimsuit and a hat. If…you feel like celebrating this with me.'

'I'll come.' She cleared her throat. 'It's wonderful news, Jarrod. I'm so happy for you.'

'For us. You're as much a part of this as I am. I'll still need you at my side at functions for a while yet. Until we've fully consolidated our position. Maybe one event each weekend from now on.' He told himself he didn't dread the day those interactions would end, that it wouldn't have mattered if she had refused to come out with him today either. Totally believed himself, too. Jarrod clenched his back molars together before he forcibly relaxed his jaw. 'I'll see you soon.'

He ended the call and waited for the results of his other calls to come through. There was a picnic basket of food, and life jackets for all of them from the marina. They'd earned this celebration. That was all. He paced the yacht. She should be here soon.

'Should I have brought champagne to smash against the hull?' The words were an attempt at lightness, but when he turned to look at her she wasn't smiling.

Her gaze was locked on him as though she didn't want to look away, as though she had missed him.

And the truth forced its way to the surface, straight past all his warnings to himself.

I have missed you, Molly, and I'm still missing you, and I don't know what to do about it.

He schooled his features, forced a smile he hoped looked natural; he glanced at Horse beside her on his lead. But his gaze soon came back to Molly. He couldn't help himself. She had a floppy hat tied with ribbon clamped on her head. White shorts revealed long, smooth legs. A breezy shirt in a dark, deep red matched the polish on her nails, and her eyes were wary, guarded and aware behind the rims of her glasses.

She was so beautiful, and he wanted her so much. In his arms, close to him, in all the ways there could be.

Sex. He wanted sex with her. Just… Yes; he was remembering that night in the tent and thinking about that. He didn't *need* anything from Molly. Didn't need to hold her against his heart, hadn't ached to do that.

'I think we should save the champagne for our celebration.' Business; if he could bring this back to the business, they could relax. Just enjoy celebrating a success. 'Come aboard. I'll tell you all about the time with the king, his investment offer.'

'You'd better. I'm dying to hear.' She made her way on board, took hold of the conversational lead.

He drew a deep breath. 'I don't think it will get too rough on the water, but as a precaution I'd recommend tying Horse to the bench seat.'

'I was thinking the same.' She led the dog in that direction.

A smile started somewhere down inside him then, and grew until he felt it curve the corners of his mouth. He *had* received a great new business account. It *was* something to celebrate, and Molly *was* here with him.

He would take those things and not think past them! 'Let's get our life jackets sorted so we can get going.'

'Okay.' She tied the lead to the bench and let him put her into her life jacket. Then laughed when he released Horse long enough to do the same to him. 'Where on earth did you get that?'

'The marina organised it for me.' He put his own jacket on with efficient movements that felt almost carefree. 'They have dog-jackets, and even cat ones, believe it or not. This is the pet equivalent of extra-extra-large size, complete with expandable straps.'

The dog woofed and wriggled a bit in his jacket, but seemed to realise this wasn't negotiable, and quickly accepted his fate.

'I'm glad you came.' Jarrod did the work to get them out to sea. Once there, he tested the yacht's speed and response under open sail. Most of all he liked seeing Molly here with him, the sea breeze blowing her hair out behind that floppy hat as she followed his directions to help him.

'I haven't done this before.' She was breathless and flushed. 'Did you really eat bugs for dinner with the king? I think you're trying to kid me about that.'

He'd told her all sorts of things about the trip, and in the middle of doing so had realised how much he wished she could have been there with him. Now he admitted the truth about the bug dinner. 'It was Moreton Bay bugs. He had them flown in especially, because he thought we might like something from our home. He seemed to enjoy them, anyway.'

'Ah. I don't know why they call that kind of lobster a bug. It's *thenus orientalis*, to be exact. Did you know the females can produce up to sixty-thousand eggs when they breed?' She flushed a little. 'Ah, well, I remember things like that. The facts.'

'Yes.' For some reason he wanted to lay her on the deck and ravish them both silly, minds and bodies.

'You—' He cleared his throat. 'You're doing a great job with the sailing.'

'Thank you.' She glanced away as though she, too, again felt the well of tension he had tried so hard to speak and ignore out of existence since he'd got her here with him this morning.

If he'd been thinking straight he would have anticipated this—Molly with him out here on a yacht, with nothing but privacy all around them. What did he think would happen? He'd told her to bring her bathing suit, for heaven's sake, had planned their trip so they could swim together. Which would mean lots of bare skin, lots of temptation.

It wasn't all about celebrating success, was it? In fact, it wasn't much about that, at all though Molly might have come along for only that reason. Or maybe not. Had her thoughts been as mixed as his? Did she want to be with him—in more than a business way?

He tried to stop the 'what ifs'. He really did.

They docked at a private mooring owned by his family. He'd considered not coming here, but the spot was tranquil.

'Oh, this is lovely.' Molly breathed the words through softly parted lips.

He wanted to kiss those lips. Maybe that fact showed in his eyes, because as their gazes locked she drew an unsteady breath, and fiddled with the ribbons of her hat as though the action was necessary to living.

'It belongs to my family.' His name was on the papers, too. 'Inherited from Grandfather Banning when he died. My parents are in town today, so we should have the place to ourselves.' A wide sandbar led to a deep, still pool. The base of the pool was rock, and an overhang of trees shaded it all.

Molly followed him as he secured the yacht and disembarked. 'Can we swim in it? I don't need to swim. In fact, maybe that's not a good idea.'

'I didn't want to make you uncomfortable today.' He never wanted to do that to her. 'This week was a long one. My parents, and the time with the king… I—I guess I missed, you know, the office and the usual routine.'

And having her there, seeing her every day. He cleared his throat. Frowned.

'I— We missed you at the office, too. Lori and me.' Molly dipped her head so her gaze was hidden from him. 'Lori's doing well. And I'm happy to be here to help celebrate, and to have a chance to go out on the yacht. That was really nice.'

'Then let's just make the rest of the day *nice*.' He called the dog to him, and tossed a tennis ball. 'Fetch, buddy.'

Horse lunged into the water with a cannonball splash. The

life jacket was balanced to keep him the right way up and, after a startled look when he hit the water, he quickly paddled after the ball.

Though her face was still conflicted, Molly covered a laugh with her hands.

It broke the tension, though it came back as they fluffed around at the edge of the water, talking about nothing, looking everywhere except at each other, until he finally took action.

His shorts doubled as swimming gear. He tugged his shirt off over his head, kicked off his deck shoes and made a bundle of them beside the water with his hat, then stepped straight in.

Through a veiled gaze, Molly watched Jarrod get in the water and suffered an instant sensory overload.

Well, no, actually the overload had started the moment she'd seen him this morning, and had stayed with her through every second of their trip while his muscles had flexed as he'd put the yacht through its paces and his gaze had come back to linger again and again on her face.

She had missed him. Way too much. Enough that when he'd invited her to join him today she had leapt at the chance before the doubts had had time to catch up with her.

Her gaze turned to her dog, and she watched Horse paddle about in the water for a moment. She could do this. Enjoy this day with Jarrod without revealing she wanted to jump all over him. Just—act calm, as though it didn't bother her to strip down to her swimsuit in front of him and get in the water with him.

Not helping, Molly!

She took her glasses off first. Maybe a slightly blurry view would help. Then the shirt, which she folded very carefully on top of Jarrod's clothes. She refused to blush that she was gathering their things together as though they belonged that way. Finally her floppy hat, her canvas shoes and then the shorts all came off.

Molly tucked their bundled things in the lee of a rock well away from the water's edge, and then got in with her gaze lowered so she wasn't looking at him at all. Not looking at that bare, wonderful chest, the broad shoulders.

An ebb of silence flowed out with the ripple of the water as she moved. When she looked up at last, he was looking at her, his gaze dark and unfathomable.

'Nice swimsuit.' He dipped his chin, and suddenly his gaze wasn't quite as unfathomable after all. 'Red—red looks good on you.'

'I don't go for revealing costumes.' Now she sounded like Miss Prissy Pants. But his gaze didn't say she looked like one.

You don't want to think about his gaze!

The two-piece suit covered all but a strip of her middle, and was sensible for being in the water. It fit like a glove, and was comfortable—that should be all that mattered, anyway.

'I put the clothes away. Yours and mine. Um, I wouldn't want Horse to take it into his head to chew on anything.' She mumbled the words.

'Molly?' He waded to her through the chest-high water at the edge of the pool.

'Y-yes?'

He took her hands gently in his and waited until she looked up at him. There was warmth in his gaze, and banked back knowledge of what they were both feeling. He looked at her over it all. 'Thank you for spending today with me. I think— I kind of needed your company.'

The tension eased out of her then, and she smiled. Her first real, unrestrained smile for the day.

With a reciprocating smile just twitching the edges of his mouth, he turned away and started to swim. 'I'm going to do laps. I plan to be faster than your dog. Do you think I will be?'

Molly laughed. And then she joined him out there in the middle of the water and swam with him, and they just kept going until finally she got too tired to go any more. Then they covered up with shirts and hats and sat on a rock shelf with their legs in the water.

Their shoulders were almost touching and, yes, she was hugely aware of that fact and their closeness. But, while they talked about this, that and the other, it didn't really seem to matter.

Horse lumbered out after a while, and came to them. They removed the life jacket, and he ran about on the sandbar, sniffing through bunches of low-growing bushes, in corners and around rocks, until Molly just had to laugh again.

'I'm glad the trip worked out for you.' She truly was. 'I hope it wasn't too awful, being there with your parents.'

'I made the choice to go.' He shrugged his shoulders, said with determined lightness, 'It was a big palace. I managed to keep my distance most of the time.'

'Jarrod…'

'Come back in the water.' He slipped back in, hat, shirt and all.

'You'll ruin your shirt. I'll bet that fabric isn't made for dunking in seawater!' She was still voicing her outrage when the first arc of water splashed straight into her face.

Molly gasped, and he laughed, and she lunged forward and splashed as much water all over him as she could manage. Their hats got soaked, their shirts got soaked; they laughed until his voice went husky from it.

And then they slung their shirts and hats on the rocks to

dry, and whiled away more time in the water as Horse continued to sniff about the sandbank.

When they returned to the yacht at last, they took turns showering in the tiny cubicle in the cabin. Molly gave Horse the can of dog food she'd brought with her, and they hosed him off on the deck.

Jarrod laughed again, his voice deep, low and rich. 'He loved us for that.'

As though to prove the point, Horse stalked away in a huff to shake his body, as though to say he resented being bathed and they'd better not try that again any time soon.

'Too-frequent baths aren't recommended for dogs. They interfere with the natural oils in their coat.' Molly spoke the words, but her pet only had half her attention. The rest remained on Jarrod. She couldn't seem to help it.

He was beautiful when he laughed. She wanted to see him happy all the time.

Freshly showered, his hair still damp and his shirt wrinkled and flopping loose around his waist, he was a lot of temptation.

'Horse can be grateful; that's the first wash he's had in a couple of weeks.' She was proud she managed to keep on with the normal conversation.

Her dog went to lie in a shady corner of the deck. Molly and Jarrod picnicked on pâté and crackers, chicken drumsticks and coleslaw and a glass each of champagne to celebrate his success with the king, while Horse snoozed with his back to them. For once her pet didn't seem interested in the idea of getting extra tidbits. Molly wondered about that for a moment, but maybe he'd worn himself out swimming and sniffing all afternoon.

She didn't want to go back, but eventually they did. They were both silent during the trip. She wondered what Jarrod was thinking. Maybe simply that he'd had a pleasant day and now he would move on to whatever was next on his agenda.

Moving on seemed to be a theme in her head lately. If only she could apply that theme a little more strongly to her emotions where her boss was concerned! But he'd said they would cut back to one social event per week, and she had managed to look enthusiastic about that. She hoped. Soon it would be no events at all, which was right where she needed things to be.

It is, Molly Taylor, and don't you forget that.

It was only when they returned the yacht to the marina and Horse didn't get up that Molly realised something was wrong with him. She should have seen it before, should have known his inactivity meant more than tiredness.

'Horse's face is swollen; his ears are an odd colour and he's breathing oddly.' She gulped over the knot of worry in her throat. Other thoughts were pushed aside as she panicked over her pet. 'I thought he was just tired. Horse. Horse!'

The dog tried to lift his head but the effort seemed too much for him.

Jarrod strode to her side. 'We need to get him to a vet.'

'I'll help carry him.' But she couldn't even get the big dog's haunches off the deck.

Jarrod pulled out his car keys and handed them to her. 'Take these and go ahead and open the rear door of the car.' He called to a man working on his craft beside them, and between them they carried the dog and settled him into the car.

'Veterinary surgery's two blocks that way.' The man pointed. 'Closed, but he lives behind it. I saw him out in the garden about half an hour ago when I drove past on my way here.'

'Thanks. I know the area.' Jarrod turned the car in that direction. 'Try not to fret, Molly. The vet will know what to do.'

'I'm concerned something might have bitten him while he was in the water.' She was anxious and blaming herself. If there hadn't been help readily available, would she and Jarrod have been able to drag the dog into the car somehow? If she hadn't been so distracted by her thoughts... 'There could have been a snake or a poisonous sea-creature.'

Jarrod glanced in the rear-view mirror and stepped down a little more on the accelerator. 'We'll find out.'

Horse made horrible harsh noises now as he tried to breathe, and his face was even more swollen. Molly fought the urge to panic outright. That wouldn't help her pet.

'The vet's here. I see him in the yard.' Jarrod drew the car to a stop.

He opened the back door while Molly waved to get the vet's attention. 'We need help.'

Molly petted Horse's poor swollen head and whispered encouragement to him as the vet approached, and then she stood back to let the man look at her pet. 'Will he be all right? We were at the beach. He swam in the water and sniffed around in the bushes. He's had a can of dog food, the same brand I always give him. We hosed him off with fresh water on the yacht after he ate.'

'Let's get him inside so I can take a better look. He's certainly a big fellow.' The vet took one end of Horse, Jarrod took the other, and they carried him very gently into the surgery by the back door.

Molly followed. She had to stop herself from thinking about the likelihood of something like this happening again when there were no others around to help her carry her dog. 'I'll buy a furniture-shifting trolley with straps, and keep it close. You can do pianos with those. Surely it would be enough for a dog!'

'Pardon?' The vet turned briefly after he and Jarrod had settled Horse on the long stainless-steel examination bench.

'Nothing. Sorry.'

'All right, let's take a look and have a bit of a chat.' The vet asked questions while he looked Horse over. Eventually, he lifted his hands away and moved to prepare a syringe. 'I don't believe he's been bitten or stung, but he is presenting classically for an allergic reaction. We'll treat it the same way we would for ourselves. Do you know how much he weighs?'

Molly told him the figure. 'I got that a month ago on a set of industrial scales at a courier place.' She'd been waiting for Izzy to finish an overtime shift one Saturday so they could ride the bus together to her mum's place.

'Excellent. That will save us having to lift him again here.' The vet prepared and administered the dose, and told them what they owed while he kept the dog under observation.

When Jarrod drew out his wallet and handed over a credit card, Molly's face heated. 'I left my things locked in the cabin on the yacht.'

'It's fine.' Jarrod waved her concern away with a flick of his hand. 'We'll sort it out later.'

The vet watched Horse to make certain the treatment was doing what it should, and then told them they could take him away. 'Keep an eye on him for the next twenty-four hours.' He handed them some pills in a small plastic packet, with information and instructions handwritten on a sticky label.

'Expect him to sleep a lot. He'll let you know when he's ready to eat and drink, and otherwise there's nothing you need to do, unless the swelling seems to be getting worse.' He gave the dog a friendly pat on the flank where he lay on the examination table. 'Now, let's get him back into the car. Will you be able to get him out at the other end?'

'If Faye and Izzy are both home maybe the three of us—'

'We're going to my cottage. It's only a few minutes' drive from here.' Jarrod spoke at the same time, and turned to face Molly with a determined expression. 'Why make him endure a long journey back to your place? We can watch him as easily here, and it's the least I can do, considering it was my idea we make this trip.'

'All right.' She nodded in agreement.

'I'll follow in my car and help unload him, then.' The vet made the decision with a brisk dip of his head.

They took care of business then, and once Horse was settled in the cottage the vet gave them his phone number and quickly left.

Evening settled as they watched over her pet. She and Jarrod ate, food he pulled from his freezer and heated in the microwave oven. Molly sat on the sofa with Horse settled on a blanket on the floor at her feet. She watched the dog's every breath.

As the evening wore on they watched her pet, and got him to take some water before he seemed to fall into deeper slumber.

They talked and sat into the night, side by side on the sofa, while the dog snored, knocked out after enough antihistamine... Well, he was a big dog.

At around ten p.m. when Horse's breathing had settled and much of the swelling had subsided, Molly realised Izzy and Faye might be worried about her. Her mum, too. 'I didn't let anyone know I wouldn't be back at my flat. I hope they haven't tried to call my phone.'

'Call them from here.' Jarrod handed her a cordless phone from an end-table beside the sofa, and she made the call.

She explained about Horse and that she had left her purse on the yacht, and asked if Izzy would mind letting Faye and her mum know she wouldn't be back until, well...

'You'll let them know when. It won't be tonight.' Jarrod inserted the words softly from beside her, and it felt so intimate to know he sat there, his arm around her shoulders. When had that happened—taking care of she and Horse and anticipating their needs before she'd managed to think them through.

'I'll let you know when I'll be back. When Horse is better enough for the trip.' Molly reassured Izzy Horse *would* be fine. She looked at her dog again and realised she believed that now. She ended the call and Jarrod put the phone away.

When he settled back he sat close to her, drew her into the shelter of his arm again. A lamp burned low on a corner table across the room.

'I've been so caught up worrying about Horse, I guess I pushed everything else aside. I didn't mean to let go so thoroughly.' Her low words were an explanation for leaning into him, maybe leaning *on* him, just a little more than she should have.

But not for staying in his hold now, though it felt so good and right to be held. Molly started to straighten.

'Don't shift away yet. It's been a good day, and then a stressful one, coming on top of an odd kind of few days for me and… Talk with me, Molly.' He murmured the words beside her ear. 'Just…about anything.'

It wasn't much of a battle to give in. She wanted to stay here, quiet, with him in the still night. When she thought she felt the brush of his lips against the hair at her temple, she shivered and subsided against him. She should do exactly the opposite.

But she was tired, she realised. Tired of fighting her feelings, and weary from concern over her dog. 'I'd rather listen while you talk. I always like…' *The sound of his voice, the knowledge he was there.*

Now, against her back, she could feel every breath he took,

the rumble of his words in his chest when he spoke. There was comfort there and Molly took it.

'What shall I talk about?' He seemed willing to indulge her, to stay in this moment with her. His fingers stroked up and down against her arm.

'What about your childhood and youth?' Had it ever been different—better? 'Did you like outdoor activities then? I know you're on a rowing team now.' Anything. She just wanted to know. Things to add to her understanding of him.

'The rowing started my first year at boarding school. I was twelve years old and liked the time on the water. Actually, I liked school. I felt I could be more myself there, you know?' A reminiscent laugh rumbled in his chest. 'I was also very clever with figures even then.'

Her heart softened. 'I can see you, all earnest and determined.'

'And a bit too resourceful there for a while. I worked out I could get access to the stock market if I did deals with boys from the oldest classes at the school. Some of them had friends who were older, university students.

'Plenty of them were interested. I charged a tidy commission for my work.' His brows knit. 'I made quite a killing, until I realised a few months later it was wrong, and stopped.'

Even then, so young, his conscience had guided him, true and sure. Despite his parents.

Molly turned her head and looked into eyes that were focused right on her. 'I wish I could have seen you then.'

'I'd rather be here with you now.' His gaze sobered, but the warmth in his eyes remained.

Molly lost herself in that gaze. She couldn't look away and from one instant to the next, just being held by him, sharing a glance with him, a knowledge flowed over her of something she had done despite promising herself she wouldn't do it.

She'd fallen in love with him. Not just a little. This was no containable, manageable crush she could rein back in.

No, this was the whole deal, and her heart shook as she accepted the truth of it—that all her struggles had led her to this—and, oh, it was frightening to know it.

'What is it? I don't want you to be sad, Molly. Is it Horse? He's going to be okay.' He raised his hand to stroke her face. A look of intensity and longing stole over his features as he searched her eyes—and there was longing for her, in some way at least.

Maybe she could have resisted somehow if not for that, but it was there, and Molly felt it deep down. She deliberately blocked off questions and concerns and let herself respond, even as something inside warned she maybe wasn't ready for this.

She knew he didn't love her. She wanted him anyway. What else was there to know? 'It's nothing. It's been a long day, as you said.'

The day she'd realised she loved him.

'Hard on you, worrying about your pet.' He pressed a kiss to her lips.

She returned the soft touch, and it went from comfort to desire so quickly.

He made a sound, then, low and yearning, and deepened the kiss.

Molly met his lips. It wasn't the same as the first time, or the last time. This was more, bigger, filled with intensity and locked into her emotions, and scary. *Because she loved him.* Because of that.

'Molly. I promised myself I'd stay away from you, but I don't know if I can.' He whispered the words nose-to-nose with her. His fingers curled around her upper arms. 'Every time I look at you or even think about you…'

'I want this.' She whispered it. 'Us, here and now, together.'

He searched her face, seemed to look deep into the heart of her. 'You need to understand I can't— I want to give you— I can only…'

She wrapped her arms around his neck. 'I want you to make love to me, Jarrod. Tonight. Just…now. I want it with—' The words 'all my heart' stayed locked inside her, but only because he mustn't know. She wasn't trying to protect herself otherwise. There was nothing she needed to be protected from.

Not your own unease? Not the fact that you've *never trusted in a deep relationship before?*

No. *His* was the unease, and Molly didn't want to think about that now either. 'I want this, you, more than anything.'

'Ah, Molly.' Jarrod held Molly to him with something edging on desperation. He hadn't meant to start this; he truly had wanted only to comfort her. And maybe he should stop this now, but she wanted him, and, God help him, he was selfish enough to reach for whatever they could have. There was an emptiness that drove him. For her, for being with her.

Tonight. Just for tonight. He swallowed something that felt like disappointment, but this was him. He couldn't be more. He stroked her arms with his fingertips. Up under the red, filmy shirt that covered the pieces of her swimsuit. Down again to fine-boned wrists he could circle with thumb and finger.

'You're so soft.' With a gentle tug of his hand, he turned her further into his arms. He wanted to be closer, so much closer than they had ever been. Something inside him needed that.

The thick-framed glasses were still perched on her nose. He lifted them away and set them on the end-table, and watched the play of thick curly lashes against her cheeks as she dropped her gaze.

Vulnerable. Shy. But then she raised her glance again, and what she wanted was there in her clouded eyes—in a swirl of so many things, but *there*—and he made a sound and crushed her to him.

She sifted her fingers through his hair as he kissed her. Cupped the back of his head with those strong, supple fingers.

Jarrod deepened the kiss, let his tongue probe the cavern of her mouth and sighed his pleasure when she followed him home again. The mixture of her eagerness and uncertainty tugged at something deep in his chest.

Was she very experienced? The thought of her with any other man burned. His muscles clenched, and he forcibly relaxed them. She'd never spoken of a boyfriend, never seemed to be dating, but would he have known? He had no right to an opinion, and nothing in his past could touch on this, on holding her close.

Her fingers stroked his skin. She pressed kisses to his neck. A different fire burned through him.

When he drew her to her feet, she met his gaze before she turned to look down at her pet.

'I don't think he needs you right now.' It was true. The dog was out to the world, and looked like staying that way, if the abandoned posture and soft snoring were any indication.

'But I do.' He admitted the truth of it even if he didn't know why, even if this would be over tomorrow. 'So much I can't think straight. So, if you want to say no to this, now is the time.' Before he lost himself completely.

No. He wouldn't do that. He still had control over his choices, could walk away right now…

The thoughts hit a wall of resistance deep inside him.

'Which one is your room?' Her hand reached for his; fingers wrapped around fingers, twined together and held on.

It was her answer, and his decision, and the relief he felt was strong. Again he wondered at the intensity, but brushed the thought away.

He wished he had rose petals to scatter before her, scented candles, and all the things, romantic things, anyone could do. Maybe they wouldn't even have meant anything, but he would have meant them with however much of him he had to give.

His bedroom faced the ocean. Filmy curtains gave privacy, but filled the room with filtered moonlight. Outside in the night, the waves of the ocean whispered against the shore. He'd never heard or felt the sound so keenly.

A pulse beat at the base of her neck. He pressed a kiss there. Her eyes drifted closed as he lifted the soft mass of her hair and spread it over his hands.

Silence fell over them then, filled with expectation and a deep familiarity. How could he know this? Yet his heart recognised each touch of her, each sigh and breath of response.

Because he *knew* her. Because they'd been together a long time, even if not in this way.

A fear of losing her rose up. He pushed it back down, because this was their moment and it had to be enough.

He asked his permission with the gentleness of his hands, with each touch and retreat, and Molly answered his silent questions with sighs and giving.

Her shirt whispered to the floor. His followed, and he peeled the upper half of her swimsuit from her body; he closed his eyes and met her lips with his as he drew her closer still.

Chest met chest, and he ached. 'Let me love you, Molly, show you...'

Molly looked into Jarrod's gaze and her heart hurt. For the

child he had been and the love that should have been his. For the man who held back from commitment, yet each touch of his hands was a gift. For the constraint inside her that she didn't understand, and all that held them apart even as they now came together.

'I want you to love me, Jarrod.' It was all she knew, and surely it was enough?

CHAPTER ELEVEN

JARROD took Molly to his bed, and laid her head against his pillows as though she were the most precious thing he had touched or seen or known. She felt that way, in this moment. His hands shook as he stripped the rest of her clothes away. A soft wonderment and gratitude filled his face as he gazed at her.

Emotion clogged Molly's throat as she returned his touch, learned each part of him—the muscular legs, flat tummy and the broadness of his chest and shoulders. The neck that tensed as she ran light fingers over his skin, and the lips that caressed hers as though he couldn't get enough of the taste of her.

A thick tide of emotion pushed at her, threatened to take her under. She pushed back, focused on *this*.

Was she imagining how this affected him because she wanted, needed, his warmth and his desire and so much more besides? Yet how could he be so gentle, so reverent, if he didn't have deeper feelings? The questions brought the struggle back, so she forced them away.

Instead she wrapped her arms around his shoulders and held him as close as she could.

Molly had had one other lover—a brief experiment a year after she'd left school while she'd worked in jobs trying to find what she wanted. He'd been nice. Someone she'd made friends with and been mildly attracted to. Maybe he'd thought the same about her before he'd gone his way.

This experience was so different. She'd never expected to have this with Jarrod. It was so much more, and maybe that explained the unease she felt inside. Yes—because her love welled so deeply she worried she wouldn't be able to keep back words. She reached her arms around him, held him close, and let the whispers be inside her mind as he finally made them one.

Jarrod hesitated then, and his gaze locked on hers and he swallowed hard. 'Molly…'

She pressed her mouth to his and told him with her kiss how much she needed, desired and wanted him. It didn't matter that she could find no words, that a churn of *something* felt locked down inside her.

His gaze settled on hers and he sought out all the closeness they could share. He led her slowly and inexorably to a dizzying precipice, and carried them over it together. She thought her heart might burst, and she couldn't seem to hold the gaze that searched her face. For a moment his emotions seemed stripped bare and she couldn't…

He tightened his arms about her. His eyelids drifted closed and his lips pressed to hers. Tears sprang to her eyes then, and she struggled to hold them back.

'Molly.' He kissed her cheeks, and she realised she had cried just a little after all.

There was hoarseness in his tone, and tenderness in the touch of his lips against her face, before he released her and padded into the bathroom.

When he returned, he slipped into the bed beside her and kissed her nose, her eyelids and her jaw. With a sigh, he drew her head into the cradle of his shoulder, tucked her body close to his and breathed in the scent of her hair.

He swallowed hard. Once. Again. 'I don't know how to thank you for what you've given me tonight, shared with me. I wish…'

He didn't finish. He didn't need to because there it was. She had known. Oh, she had known.

'I should check on Horse.' And gather her things and find a way to leave, even if it meant persuading a taxi to take her, and rousing Izzy and Faye to help with her dog. Deep exhaustion pulled at her as she uttered the words.

'Let me check on him.' Jarrod rose from the bed and tugged open a drawer. Moments later he had donned boxer shorts. He handed her an oversized T-shirt, and his face was guarded as he left the room.

Molly let him go and, when she was alone in the room, tugged the T-shirt over her head and the sheet up to her chin, and closed her eyes in a ridiculous attempt to blot out the troubled feeling inside her chest.

Then his arms were around her again, his body warm against hers, and he sighed as though from deep down in his soul.

'If Horse needs me…' Her words were slurred with the beginnings of a bone-deep sleep.

'I'll make sure you know if he needs you.' He curved his body protectively around hers—and later she would examine that, but now she couldn't—and she slept.

Morning came with a slow awakening—the murmur of Jarrod's voice somewhere in the house, a muffled woof of response from her dog. Horse sounded better. Molly realised that fact before the deep tension rolled through her.

Then it did, and she sucked in a sharp breath and held it as her fingers tightened on the sheet that covered her.

She and Jarrod had made love. She would *not* regret that, yet…

He'd made it clear he couldn't truly love her. That last night couldn't be more. Molly had to acknowledge that, make it clear she wouldn't look for more.

Her things from the yacht were inside the bedroom door, her clothes laundered and waiting for her on the end of the bed, her glasses on the beside table.

How long had he been up, taking care of things for her? Maybe getting people to run errands on her behalf. Those small kindnesses almost pushed her over the edge, but she couldn't go there now. Not yet. Molly showered and dressed.

They were in the kitchen. Horse was on his feet, eating dog food off a plate on the floor with a reassuring amount of enthusiasm. His face was back to normal size, his breathing good.

Jarrod stood at the sink with a cup of something in his hand. His back was turned to her, and she gave herself just one brief moment to look before she pushed it all down.

'He's going to be okay, despite my inability to take care of his needs at the time.' The observation was a little tight. She hoped Jarrod would blame that on her concerns for her dog. Molly forced herself further into the room, gave Horse a pat on the head and let him get back to his eating.

'You took care of him just fine.' Jarrod turned away from his position at the window, and, oh, there was so much conflict in his eyes. 'Last night you gave me something precious. I never expected us to be together that way, and I don't want you to think—'

'I don't. I don't think anything.'

That it should be more, that he could give her what her heart needed, when he'd always made it clear that wouldn't happen? No.

He cleared his throat, made an uneasy gesture with his hand. 'Would you like coffee, some cereal or toast?'

'Not right now.' She didn't want to make a pretence of eating. 'Actually, now Horse is on the mend, I need to arrange to get him back to my flat. I'd still like to watch him today, if I can have the day off work.'

The words brought the parameters of their true relationship back into focus. She was his PA. He was her boss.

That was *safe*.

For *him*. He believed he needed those boundaries. Yet hadn't she kept a boundary between herself and the world too? By always holding back a part of her from her mum and the others because they dared to dream and they wouldn't face the reality of their futures?

No. That was ridiculous. Molly worried about them. She didn't resent them.

Don't you?

'I can take care of things at the office, and Lori will be there in the afternoon.' He took a step towards her. Then stopped, and his face tightened, all the planes and angles that had softened last night as he'd held her in his arms. 'Stay here with Horse. There's no need to move him just yet. When I get back, I can drive you both to your flat.'

Molly didn't want him to drive her, didn't want to stay here, either. Didn't want the turn of her thoughts, when she needed to know at least that the other relationships that mattered in her life were fine.

Just fine!

Most of all she wanted him to go so she could start to pull herself back together. 'I appreciate that, and I think I might have that coffee after all, but I can get it myself. In a moment. I'd like to give Horse some attention first.'

His brows drew down and he looked torn.

So she made it all clear, put it into words so he could have no doubt she understood. 'We both knew last night couldn't be more.' She was grateful for Horse's thick fur beneath her fingertips, and the press of his warm body against her side. Grateful for the relief of saying it.

Molly buried her fingers in that fur, though she forced herself to look up and meet Jarrod's gaze as she went on. 'We let last night happen. It's done and can't be undone, but now we have to put it behind us.'

'I don't regret it, Molly. What we shared. In fact—I don't know—I'm wondering if— I don't want to lose…' He cut himself off. His jaw tightened and for just a moment regret and frustration showed in his eyes, as though he wanted to fight this.

Hope and that uncertain dread filled her chest again.

But it was a blink in time. As long as it took for him to shutter his expression, to draw back. 'Well, I know that can't work, and it's not as if you…'

Loved him? Yes; she did.

So why are you desperate to get away from this instead of demanding he try harder, try to give more?

Because he won't, all right? He would not give her that, and she had every right to keep herself back.

Horse lumbered back to the blanket in the living room. Molly followed him, and, since Jarrod was showered and dressed, she figured he would get ready and quickly leave.

He did so, with last-minute instructions to call him if she needed anything, anything at all.

When she thanked him and assured him she wouldn't need a thing, he hesitated, looked at her with his fists clenched at his sides, and then he finally left.

Molly cleared up all signs of her stay, and of Horse's stay from her boss's home, phoned for a taxi, and was soon back in her flat with her pet. She hadn't paid Jarrod yet for the vet's bill, but she would take care of that.

She would take care of everything. Somehow.

Jarrod stared out of his office window and rubbed at the tight spot above his ribs. It had begun when he'd woken first thing this morning with Molly held protectively in his arms, their night together ended. It hadn't let up since.

He'd wanted to stay with her this morning. Had wanted to make rash promises. Anything to be with her, to hold on to the delight and the intimacy, and so much more that had no words.

Instead he'd left, and that had cost him, more than he could comprehend. For the first time in years, the wall Jarrod had built against his parents' lack of feeling towards him—around his conviction a committed relationship was not for him because of their example, of their blood running through his veins—had shaken.

He could have protected Molly, made sure it hadn't gone where it had last night. The thought brought a fierce internal rebuttal. How could he wish away what they had shared? But how much would it hurt her now?

And you.

He wanted to deny that, yet in the dark hours of the night he had wanted to keep her in all the ways there were.

Jarrod didn't know what to do, how to have what he wanted. So he tried to ignore it all. He buried himself in work and held off until almost lunchtime before he phoned the cottage. He would check on Horse's progress. Make it sensible.

She wasn't there. He acknowledged it way deep down inside him as the call finished ringing out. Well, had he really expected her to stay?

While he sat there and stared at the phone, it rang.

It was Molly. 'I'm back at my flat. Horse was doing well enough, and I found a taxi to take us. I thought he should be where he feels safe and familiar, and he seems happier, all but back to normal.'

As Molly was happier in her own home, putting distance between them now? What did he want? That she should have waited at his cottage so he could have taken her away at the end of his working day? What difference did it make when she left or how? The result was the same, the one he'd known from the start had to happen. The knowledge hurt more than he'd thought it could.

'I'm glad Horse is feeling better.' He rubbed that spot on his chest again.

The other phone line began to ring. She must have heard it, for she spoke quickly. 'It sounds like you're busy, and Lori won't be there for an hour yet, and Horse needs checking-on again. I just wanted to let you know I'd moved him. I'll let you go. Goodbye.' She ended the call.

Jarrod answered the call perhaps more curtly than he could have. '*Banning.*'

'If this is a bad time…'

Jarrod drew a deep breath and blew it out again. 'Mrs Armiga. I hadn't expected to hear from you. You haven't responded to my phone messages.'

'I received them all, and I admired your efforts, and so now I want to give you another chance rather than simply pulling my investments.'

'That's good news. Thank you.' He said the words by rote. She'd been the last holdout, the one still on the fence, refusing to jump one way or the other.

Right now Jarrod found it hard even to care that the woman finally seemed willing to talk. And *nothing* felt right. 'Well,

I'm pleased, and thank you very much for letting me know. I'll get Molly—one of my *assistants*—to phone you and organise an appointment.'

'I discussed this with my sons, and they called a family meeting, and they're prepared to meet with you this evening.' Mrs Armiga went on, steel behind the pleasant words. 'You can get to Adelaide in time for dinner, yes? That's where I am, with my eldest and the others. Visiting, you understand.'

Adelaide for dinner. At the other end of the country far away from Molly, without seeing her until he got back whatever time tomorrow—which wouldn't be the start of the day, that was for sure.

Every part of Jarrod wanted to say no, he wouldn't go—that the woman and her sons could come to him for this discussion, or skip it altogether, and too bad if he lost her business.

But would it be any easier for Molly to come back to work tomorrow and have to face him straight away? And maybe he needed time to figure out his feelings a little better. That aching void that loving with her had only partly filled.

'I'll be there. Give me a time and place to meet with you and your sons.' He paused. 'I'll be leaving again on the first plane back to Brisbane tomorrow.'

'You're committed to your business.' A grudging approval.

Jarrod made the trip. He schmoozed the woman and impressed her sons. By the end of the evening, his client was convinced she could trust him with her business. The sons were happy. Everyone was happy. Jarrod apparently was no longer 'too smooth'.

So, great. Except Jarrod wasn't happy. Molly hadn't been able to meet his gaze after their loving. He'd tried not to remember that, but why hadn't she?

Because you told her it was one night. It wasn't enough.

And what if he now wanted to give more, desperately wanted to do that? He tossed and turned the night away in a hotel bed and got to the airport far too early for his flight.

He returned to the office, headed straight there from the airport determined to tell her…?

Jarrod hadn't known what, and then he walked in and Lori was there, because it was her full day today, but Molly wasn't. The older woman lifted her head from her work and told him Molly had taken a leave of absence, and pointed him to a sealed note on his desk.

The message was short. She'd gone away because she needed to think, and he didn't need to worry because the work was in good hands with Lori.

It wasn't a resignation, or a guarantee Molly would be back. A match for his own uncertainty, then—but, if so, why did it feel wrong to him? Not undecided—*wrong*.

Lori stood in the doorway of the office. 'If you need me to work full-time hours for a while, I can.'

Could she make Molly come back and things return to how they'd been before he'd driven his PA away with his stupidity, his selfishness and his lack? Could she stop Molly's hurt? Because deep inside he knew that hurt was there, and he'd made it happen, and that was the worst of all.

'Thank you, Lori. That will help.' Jarrod folded the note, folded it again, and tucked it into the pocket of his shirt over his heart.

He had no right to try to hold Molly, because he had none of the things to give her that she needed and deserved to have. That was what he'd always believed, wasn't it?

And what was there to make him believe anything had changed?

CHAPTER TWELVE

MOLLY breathed, worked, went on. One day after another, over and over and, if her heart didn't feel any better—if she longed for Jarrod and couldn't begin to forget him—what could she do? There was no point thinking about him any more, wishing for the moon.

Cinderella had got the moon, or at least the glass slippers and the Prince. Molly Taylor had had one wonderful night and an ache inside her heart.

It was afternoon, a beautiful Tasmanian day, cool enough that Molly wore long trousers and a lightweight cardigan over her strawberry-red blouse. Bright colours were meant to cheer. So what if the rest of the outfit was black and far more suited to her mood? Molly happened to like black. It was practical.

But liking things and thinking about her clothing wouldn't help her do what she had to do. She looked out over the bluff at the ocean, and acknowledged it was time to take the next step. One that would take her out of Jarrod Banning's orbit fully and permanently.

Oh, she had come here to think, and a part of her had hoped she could go back. But who was she kidding to believe she could return to Jarrod, keep working for him, as though nothing had happened? She'd known all along she couldn't afford to become closer to him. She had tried to make herself believe otherwise, but that initial belief was now even stronger.

Molly swallowed hard. The sea-wind blew in her face, but it wasn't the reason for the sudden rush of moisture to her eyes. Her love for her boss was responsible for that.

Unrequited love. Don't forget that.

Jarrod had loved her as much as he could—with his body. With affection. He couldn't help it if he was trapped by a lifetime of poor family history that stopped him from giving more.

Convenient thoughts, Molly. Just as though you don't have any family history to contend with.

Her recent conversation with her mother came back to her. Anna had phoned Molly at Visi's estate here a number of times—concerned for her daughter, for the sudden change of direction in Molly's life that Molly hadn't wanted to elaborate on—until finally she had told Anna.

'I fell in love with Jarrod, Mum, but he wasn't prepared to love me back.'

Anna had fallen silent, and then had sighed into the phone. *'There's no choice about love, Molly. It just happens.'*

Well, love hadn't happened for Jarrod. A part of Molly had hoped for more against all the odds anyway. Had hoped Jarrod would come after her, or phone to check on her, perhaps pull rank and say she owed it to the company to go back. She'd told Lori her destination. Jarrod would only have had to ask.

But she'd heard nothing. Her text messages and phone calls had been from Izzy, Faye and her mum.

Molly kicked at the turf at her feet. What she needed to do was tell Terrence she was done with the grunt work, that he could work on the library upgrade at his leisure now, or employ a whole team to work on it. She needed to pack up her suitcase and go...

Somewhere. To a job at Allonby's company, if the man still had one on offer. Was Brisbane large enough to hold Molly and Jarrod and allow her to get on with her life without thinking of him constantly, wishing things could have been different?

Well, they weren't different.

A footfall sounded behind her, and Molly dashed her fingers across her cheeks and drew a deep breath. She'd thought herself alone out here, that Visi was absorbed in his afternoon routine: the magnate in the counting house, counting out his money.

She doubted he really had gold stored under the house. And she really needed to stop with the off-kilter fairy-tale analogies. Yet Visi was a man very much alone.

The difference was he seemed happy that way. Maybe one day Molly would be like that.

Molly tried to smile as she turned around to face the man who had accepted her offer to work in his library, using the software package they'd emailed each other about.

The smile turned to frozen shock, to a hard hammering of her heart against her ribs, as she recognised...

'Jarrod.' She should have known the sound of his step. She *did* know it. If she hadn't been so distracted, she would have realised straight away this was not Visi, but her boss.

No. Not her boss any more. Not anything to her, nor she to him.

Yet her gaze searched his face, soaked up each facet of his appearance. The beige business trousers, the dark-navy shirt with the collar open at the neck. No tie. Ruffled hair that looked as if he'd run his fingers through it. His gaze bored into hers as though he needed to look, to take all of her in at once.

'What are you doing here? Is everything all right at the office?'

'The office is running smoothly enough. You made a good choice when you appointed Lori. The investments are doing well.' He took a step towards her. Just one.

'Is it your parents, then? Have they caused you more trouble?' Why couldn't they just leave Jarrod alone, if they weren't prepared to love him as they should, with full and un-conditional love?

Like you've always given, Molly?

'I'm not here because of my parents.' This time, when he moved, it was to step close enough that she could have reached out and touched him—oh, so easily.

Instead Molly locked her arms about her waist and didn't move them—because if she did that she might just wrap those arms right around him and want to hold on. 'I know I aban-doned my commitment to you, to the business.'

'And I'd like you to come back.' The words came out in a low growl of sound. 'I want that, Molly, you back working at my side.' He reached for her hand and held it.

Just a clasp of fingers against fingers. How could it make her heart ache so? But that touch reminded her of the way he had loved her. As if with his heart, even though that wasn't the case. Molly's fingers curled about his. She should let go, tell him she couldn't return. Not ever.

'Has Visi offered you a permanent position here with him? He wouldn't tell me when I arrived.'

'I'm ready to leave here. The groundwork is done. It was only ever going to be that.' Just a few loose ends to tidy. Not even that, really.

She glanced again at the churning sea below them. 'This was never meant to be more than a stopgap, a chance to think and straighten out my plans, but I can't—'

'Then there's still hope.' His hand tightened over hers.

Molly started to shake her head, but he took a deep breath and began to speak.

'I've told you I still want to work with you. That's up to you and, if you decide you don't want to do that any more, I'll have to accept it.'

'You don't have to say—'

'Yes, I do. I have to say I want you…in other ways.' He brought her hand to his chest, flattened the palm there so she felt the beat of his heart beneath her fingertips, the warmth of his hand above hers.

He'd held her in that way before. Molly's breath caught. She wanted him to lower his head, to kiss her, wanted to forget this couldn't work.

She shored up her defences instead, before they crumpled completely. 'I tried to step over a line, to take more than I can have. It didn't work; I always knew it wouldn't, but for a time I let myself pretend.'

It was true.

'What if I said I believe it *can* work? I've thought about many things, Molly—about the two of us, about how we were when we shared that night at my cottage.' He drew a slow, deep breath, and eased it out again. 'We were special together, and I don't think we should throw that away.'

Oh, she wanted the chance to be with him again, but for how long? And how much more would it hurt when he finally gave up on her, as he most surely would?

'Jarrod.' She broke away from him, turned to stare out at the relentless sea—the vastness of a force that couldn't be contained or reckoned with, it simply *was*. 'I can't—'

'Please. Give me a chance to tell you.' His words were low and fierce behind her. 'I didn't know what love was. There hadn't been a whole lot of it in my life, and I thought

I couldn't feel it—but when you went away I thought something inside me had died. I couldn't think or function properly. All I could do was miss you and wish you weren't gone.'

'Don't.' She swung to face him. *Don't tempt me when I can't be tempted any more and survive it. Don't make me believe you might love me.* 'You just…missed me. I was a good PA, and we became close.'

'I made love to you and I gave my heart to you. That was new to me and I didn't understand at the time. I thought our being together wouldn't change me, that nothing could.' He broke off, swallowed. 'But I've realised I can't hold back on loving you, Molly. I don't want to hold back any more, and I *can* love you, because it's all there in my heart, and I hope I haven't lost you by taking this long to see.'

He crushed her hands in his and probably didn't realise he'd done it. 'I want a chance to love you, Molly. That night at the cottage was the best of my life. Not only because it was the night you gave yourself to me, but because that's what I've wanted for so long even though I didn't realise it—that togetherness that's so much more.'

He drew a deep breath. 'With you.'

'A working-class girl and a multi-millionaire from one of the wealthiest and most prestigious families in Queensland?' She barely knew what she was saying. Couldn't think.

'Billionaire by right of inheritance from my grandfather, in my own right as well.' He lifted his hand. So much braver than her.

'I can't change where I came from, Molly. I'll always be what I am—and I admit I like having wealth, to indulge in building a yacht if I want to, to buy you all the latest things you want to try out in the office. I'm asking you to accept there's more to me than my history, and that all of me loves you, despite telling you that couldn't happen.'

She wanted so very much to believe. 'Jarrod, I—'

He'd said he loved her, that he'd realised his capability for those feelings. For her. That he'd found a way past his road-blocks. If she believed it.

If she believed, she had to love him back. And she had suppressed her love behind a wall of uncertainty and caution and refused to believe or reach out. Now, there was no reason not to. Nothing but the fears and hurts and constraints she'd held onto.

'I didn't expect this, that you'd come. I hoped—' Her words burst out and her gaze locked with his.

'I had to come for you. I want a chance to be part of a family where love is what matters.' He laid his heart bare to her. 'I want to live with you, love you, go to margarita birthdays, eat home-made cake and play Scrabble games with you and your mum and the others, and cook for you while you make special blinds for our home. I want it all. Tell me that's possible, that you need and want it as much as I do?'

Molly wanted to tell Jarrod exactly that. Oh, she *needed* to tell him. 'I've been so wrong, so ready to say I knew it all and had all the answers when I never had a clue. I love you, Jarrod. I have for a long time, even while I felt angry at Mum and the others and never fully let myself love them.'

He went to take her into his arms, but she shook her head.

Instead, he spoke. 'I've seen you all together. They love you, and I know you love them. I don't understand what you're trying to say.'

'And you're so much more generous than I am!' Molly forced herself to face that. 'You've managed to love, despite your parents' long-standing coldness towards you. I've had everything, *everything*—three women who have loved me without measure, no matter what—and I…haven't loved them back enough.'

Tears pricked her eyes as she admitted it. 'Instead, I've blamed them for being frivolous, have been unkind about their dreams. They've given me so much love and care, without me doing a thing to deserve it other than existing. I should have let them enjoy their lives however they wanted.'

He dipped his head close to hers. 'What were you afraid of?'

'That I wouldn't be able to support them all through their retirement years, that they would need help and I wouldn't have enough resources to see them through.'

Gentle hands squeezed her shoulders. 'Those sound like valid worries. If they haven't taken care to save money…'

'They haven't, but that's no excuse for me being intolerant and judgemental of the people who dropped everything to love me—and still would, any time they thought I needed them.' Molly would make up for that. Somehow she would. 'I'll find a way to cover them, and I'll stop going on about it. They can holiday where they like—fly to the Bahamas if they can scrimp the money together for it.'

'Then maybe you do need to forgive yourself and them, as I have to forgive my parents for not loving me.' His expression softened as his gaze held hers. 'I think I'll have to go on forgiving them for a long time, and maybe that means I need to forgive myself, too, because I've resented the hell out of them for as long as I can remember. Don't kid yourself otherwise, Molly.'

His honesty humbled her, made her heart soar and ache all at once.

And Molly let go at last. 'I love you, Jarrod. I love you with all of my heart and spirit, and body and soul. If you truly want me—'

'I do. Oh, Molly, I do.' He kissed her then. A long, beautiful, loving kiss that filled her heart until she thought she might burst, and then filled it all over again.

He wrapped her body close to his, sighed his relief and pleasure against her hair while the sea breeze wafted around them and the waves ebbed and flowed below.

'It may not be easy,' he warned her. 'I plan to remain in business in Brisbane for the rest of my working life, and that means butting up against my parents, even if only socially from time to time, whether they ever accept my choices or not.'

'They won't hurt us. We won't let them.' Because Molly *would* draw Jarrod into her family, with Anna, Faye, Izzy and Horse, and she would watch out for him and give him all the love she had unwittingly held back.

Love in the fullest measure. 'Um, can you manage having a woolly mammoth for a pet? He's waiting back at my flat for me, and I've missed him so much, and he's really very good despite being a bit silly.'

'Horse is yours.' As far as Jarrod was concerned, that seemed to settle it. His face softened as he gazed at her. 'You're going to marry me. Soon.'

'Yes.' Her heart filled with such love, she struggled to contain it.

'Then do you think we could go home to Brisbane now?' He caught her against the shelter of his body, breathed in the scent of her hair, closed his eyes and opened them, and his love was revealed again. 'I, uh, I chartered a jet to get here because I didn't want to have to wait if you somehow said yes. I was determined to take you back with me.'

There was a hint of apology in his tone, and she smiled. 'A charter flight will be good. We'll get there sooner.'

'I want to help with your family's finances, too.' He said

it cautiously, as though concerned she might rebuff the offer. 'I know I've been pushy about money, insisting you take more for your change in duties—but I *have* it, and you deserved it, and if I can use some of it to ease your mind…'

'Thank you.' For his generosity and his understanding and for being this man she loved so much. 'I'd like to look into that with you. Maybe we could plan some investment for them?'

'That would be my pleasure. I've wanted to run a portfolio for you since you started to work for me.' He hesitated. 'I can't think of any investment I'd like to do more than for *my* family.'

She wrapped her arms around his waist and hugged hard, felt the tremble in his hands as they closed around her in response. 'I want to show you I can be as generous in loving you. It's our love that counts more than anything.' She truly understood that at last.

They linked arms and retraced their steps towards Terrence Visi's mansion home. Jarrod turned to look at her. 'I want to romance you properly when we get back. With a candlelit dinner on the yacht, and fine wine, and a ring.'

Her heart swelled with love for him. 'I love you so much.'

A lot still remained. Would she continue to work with Jarrod in her previous capacity? Or as she had done when they'd sought to end the rumours that had drawn he and Molly ultimately closer in the end and had strengthened his business even more, for all his mother had tried to do?

Where would they live? Probably not in her apartment between Izzy and Faye. Maybe they would commute between his apartment and the seaside cottage, or even move into a home in the suburbs so they could start a family? Molly's face heated at the thought, and Jarrod looked down at her.

His gaze darkened with intrigued interest. 'What are you thinking?'

'Of how much I want to be in your arms again, as we were that night at your cottage, and that maybe one day we might…have children.'

'Children.' He stilled, and his gaze darkened even more. 'Have I said how much I love you, Molly Taylor?'

She returned his smile, loved him so much. 'You might have mentioned it.'

'Good.' He caught her hand in his and led her towards the hire-car that stood in her host's driveway. 'Then you'll understand if I whisk you away right now and get Visi to send your things on to you.' His voice deepened. 'I need you to myself.'

She smiled into eyes that shone with love for her. 'I love you, Jarrod Banning, exactly as you are, in all the ways you are. I'm ready to show you just how much I mean that.'

'And I love you just as much.'

He tucked her into the car and they drove away. Straight into a future where they would do their best to indeed make all their dreams come true.

It appeared this Cinderella had found her happy ending after all.

* * * * *

*Celebrate 60 years of pure reading pleasure
with Harlequin®!*

*Harlequin Romance® is celebrating by showering you with
DIAMOND BRIDES in February 2009.
Six stories that promise to bring a touch of sparkle to your
life, with diamond proposals and dazzling weddings,
sparkling brides and gorgeous grooms!*

*Enjoy a sneak peek at Caroline Anderson's
TWO LITTLE MIRACLES,
available February 2009 from Harlequin Romance®.*

'I'VE FOUND HER.'

Max froze.

It was what he'd been waiting for since June, but now—now he was almost afraid to voice the question. His heart stalling, he leaned slowly back in his chair and scoured the investigator's face for clues. 'Where?' he asked, and his voice sounded rough and unused, like a rusty hinge.

'In Suffolk. She's living in a cottage.'

Living. His heart crashed back to life, and he sucked in a long, slow breath. All these months he'd feared—

'Is she well?'

'Yes, she's well.'

He had to force himself to ask the next question. 'Alone?'

The man paused. 'No. The cottage belongs to a man called John Blake. He's working away at the moment, but he comes and goes.'

God. He felt sick. So sick he hardly registered the next few words, but then gradually they sank in. 'She's got *what?*'

'Babies. Twin girls. They're eight months old.'

'Eight—?' he echoed under his breath. 'They must be his.'

He was thinking out loud, but the P.I. heard and corrected him. 'Apparently not. I gather they're hers. She's been there since mid-January last year, and they were born during the summer—June, the woman in the post office thought. She was more than helpful. I think there's been a certain amount of speculation about their relationship.'

He'd just bet there had. God, he was going to kill her. Or Blake. Maybe both of them.

'Of course, looking at the dates, she was presumably pregnant when she left you, so they could be yours, or she could have been having an affair with this Blake character before…'

He glared at the unfortunate P.I. 'Just stick to your job. I can do the math,' he snapped, swallowing the unpalatable possibility that she'd been unfaithful to him before she'd left. 'Where is she? I want the address.'

'It's all in here,' the man said, sliding a large envelope across the desk to him. 'With my invoice.'

'I'll get it seen to. Thank you.'

'If there's anything else you need, Mr Gallagher, any further information—'

'I'll be in touch.'

'The woman in the post office told me Blake was away at the moment, if that helps,' he added quietly, and opened the door.

Max stared down at the envelope, hardly daring to open it, but when the door clicked softly shut behind the P.I., he eased up the flap, tipped it and felt his breath jam in his throat as the photos spilled out over the desk.

Oh, lord, she looked gorgeous. Different, though. It took him a moment to recognise her, because she'd grown her hair, and it was tied back in a ponytail, making her look younger and somehow freer. The blond highlights were gone, and it was back to its natural soft golden-brown, with a little curl in the end of the ponytail that he wanted to thread his finger through and tug, just gently, to draw her back to him.

Crazy. She'd put on a little weight, but it suited her. She looked well and happy and beautiful, but oddly, considering how desperate he'd been for news of her for the past year— one year, three weeks and two days, to be exact—it wasn't only Julia who held his attention after the initial shock. It was the babies sitting side by side in a supermarket trolley. Two identical and absolutely beautiful little girls.

* * * * *

When Max Gallagher hires a P.I. to find his estranged wife, Julia, he discovers she's not alone—she has twin baby girls, and they might be his. Now workaholic Max has just two weeks to prove that he can be a wonderful husband and father to the family he wants to treasure.

Look for TWO LITTLE MIRACLES by Caroline Anderson, available February 2009 from Harlequin® Romance.

CELEBRATE
60 YEARS
OF PURE READING PLEASURE
WITH HARLEQUIN®!

We'll be spotlighting a different series
every month throughout 2009
to celebrate our 60th anniversary.

Look for Harlequin® Romance in February!

DIAMOND BRIDES

**Harlequin® Romance is celebrating by showering
you with Diamond Brides in February 2009.**

Six stories that promise to bring a touch of sparkle to
your life, with diamond proposals and dazzling weddings,
sparkling brides and gorgeous grooms!

Collect all six books in February 2009,
featuring *Two Little Miracles* by Caroline Anderson.

*Look for the Diamond Brides miniseries
in February 2009!*

REQUEST YOUR FREE BOOKS!
2 FREE NOVELS PLUS 2
FREE GIFTS!

From the Heart, For the Heart

YES! Please send me 2 FREE Harlequin Romance® novels and my 2 FREE gifts (gifts are worth about $10). After receiving them, if I don't wish to receive any more books, I can return the shipping statement marked "cancel". If I don't cancel, I will receive 4 brand-new novels every month and be billed just $3.32 per book in the U.S. or $3.80 per book in Canada, plus 25¢ shipping and handling per book and applicable taxes, if any*. That's a savings of over 15% off the cover price! I understand that accepting the 2 free books and gifts places me under no obligation to buy anything. I can always return a shipment and cancel at any time. Even if I never buy another book, the two free books and gifts are mine to keep forever.

114 HDN ERQW   314 HDN ERQ9

Name	(PLEASE PRINT)	

Address		Apt. #

City	State/Prov.	Zip/Postal Code

Signature (if under 18, a parent or guardian must sign)

Mail to the **Harlequin Reader Service:**
IN U.S.A.: P.O. Box 1867, Buffalo, NY 14240-1867
IN CANADA: P.O. Box 609, Fort Erie, Ontario L2A 5X3

Not valid to current subscribers of Harlequin Romance books.

Want to try two free books from another line?
Call 1-800-873-8635 or visit www.morefreebooks.com.

* Terms and prices subject to change without notice. N.Y. residents add applicable sales tax. Canadian residents will be charged applicable provincial taxes and GST. Offer not valid in Quebec. This offer is limited to one order per household. All orders subject to approval. Credit or debit balances in a customer's account(s) may be offset by any other outstanding balance owed by or to the customer. Please allow 4 to 6 weeks for delivery. Offer available while quantities last.

Your Privacy: Harlequin Books is committed to protecting your privacy. Our Privacy Policy is available online at www.eHarlequin.com or upon request from the Reader Service. From time to time we make our lists of customers available to reputable third parties who may have a product or service of interest to you. If you would prefer we not share your name and address, please check here.

You're invited to join our Tell Harlequin Reader Panel!

By joining our new reader panel you will:

- Receive Harlequin® books—they are FREE and yours to keep with no obligation to purchase anything!
- Participate in fun online surveys
- Exchange opinions and ideas with women just like you
- Have a say in our new book ideas and help us publish the best in women's fiction

In addition, you will have a chance to win great prizes and receive special gifts!
See Web site for details. Some conditions apply.
Space is limited.

To join, visit us at
www.TellHarlequin.com.

HARLEQUIN *Romance*

Coming Next Month

It's Harlequin's 60th anniversary this year!
Harlequin Romance® is celebrating with diamond proposals and
dazzling weddings, sparkling brides and gorgeous grooms as we
shower you with *Diamond Brides* this month!

#4075 THE AUSTRALIAN'S SOCIETY BRIDE Margaret Way
Diamond Brides

Boyd Blanchard is the most eligible bachelor in Australia, and way out of
Leona's league. But Boyd secretly longs to make Leona his. When the
Blanchard family diamonds go missing, Leona takes the blame for her
brother's mistake. And when Boyd discovers her secret, he blackmails the
vivacious redhead into being his diamond bride!

#4076 HER VALENTINE BLIND DATE Raye Morgan
Diamond Brides

On Valentine's Day, waitress Cari is literally swept off her feet by a tall, dark,
devastatingly handsome stranger. By the time Max realizes Cari isn't his blind
date, it's too late! He's already falling for the woman who's brought a touch of
sparkle to this billionaire's life.

#4077 THE ROYAL MARRIAGE ARRANGEMENT Rebecca Winters
Diamond Brides

Alexandra has come to the famous House of Savoy to sell her mother's
diamonds and erase her debts, only to be told the diamonds are fake! A
convenient marriage to Italian prince Lucca might be the solution to her
problems, but Alex can't help wishing his feelings for her were real.

#4078 TWO LITTLE MIRACLES Caroline Anderson
Diamond Brides

Julia's husband Max is back, after a year's absence, to put things right
between them. But there are two small surprises waiting for him: twin baby
girls! Max has just two weeks to prove he can be a wonderful husband and
father to the family he treasures.

#4079 MANHATTAN BOSS, DIAMOND PROPOSAL Trish Wylie
Diamond Brides

Tycoon playboy Quinn doesn't believe in love, until he hires secretary Clare.
She's rocked him to the core, but after being jilted at the altar, Clare keeps her
heart guarded. Can Quinn convince her to say "yes" to his diamond proposal?

#4080 THE BRIDESMAID AND THE BILLIONAIRE Shirley Jump
Diamond Brides

The only thing billionaire Kane can't afford is a happy-ever-after, so he's
escaping stifling New York to experience an ordinary life for a while. But when
he falls for bridesmaid Susanna, Kane's about to discover that life with this
rare beauty will be anything but ordinary!